...areer with *The D...*
...st Medical Romance, *I...*
p...ished, and with more than 20 ...
s...s enjoyed writing ever since.

BACHELOR DOC, UNEXPECTED DAD

DIANNE DRAKE

MILLS & BOON

Published in Great Britain 2018
by Mills & Boon, an imprint of HarperCollins*Publishers*
1 London Bridge Street, London, SE1 9GF

© 2018 Dianne Despain

ISBN: 978-0-263-93367-3

MIX
Paper from
responsible sources
FSC® C007454

This book is produced from independently certified FSC™ paper
to ensure responsible forest management.
For more information visit www.harpercollins.co.uk/green.

Printed and bound in Spain
by CPI, Barcelona

To a real-life cowboy I met on a lonely ranch road.
Thanks for the inspiration!

PROLOGUE

MATT ROLLED OVER in bed and looked at her. She was still sleeping, and so beautiful in her sleep he wanted to stay another night with her. That wasn't his life, though. As tempting as Ellie was, and she was the most tempting woman he'd ever met, he didn't get to have that kind of involvement in his life. In fact, he'd planned everything to fit him the way he wanted—no strings. It was easier. People didn't get hurt.

Still, that graceful form under the satin sheets next to him was so hard to resist. And it wasn't just the physical intimacy that had been good. They'd talked. Dined. Danced. Things he'd never done with a woman before. And Ellie was so easy just to hold, to be near.

The first night, he'd assumed it would be fun and games, she'd be gone by the time he went to sleep, and he would never see her again. But that's not what had happened. They'd stood on the balcony for a while, looking at the beautiful Reno lights, laughing at silly things, talking much longer than he'd expected to. And the night had passed so quickly. In fact, by the time they'd gotten around to what he'd assumed would take only a short time, the sun had already been coming up and he'd been wondering where the night had gone.

Then Matt had watched Ellie, off and on that day, always having an excuse to be near her. It was a convention and medical conference after all. The hotel ballroom was filled with various displays of new medical products and pharmaceuticals. Somehow, the ones that had seemed to catch his attention had always been near her booth. And while he'd tried not to be obvious about watching her, Ellie had caught him at it a time or two, leaving him with a blush on his face and a shrug on his shoulder. Much the way a schoolboy with a crush would act.

But those looks she'd caught—they'd led to a second night, one with much less talking and much more passion. In fact, she had already been in his bed when he'd gone back to his room, having bribed a maid to let her in. And that night it had been like two desperate people clinging together at the end of the world. In some ways, that's what it was. The end of their little world as, in three days' time, he'd be back in a hospital in Mosul, putting pieces of injured soldiers back together. That's who Matt was. And that was his world. Not this one.

Still, as Matt buttoned his shirt and headed to the hotel room door that second morning he wondered if something like this, someone like Ellie, could ever have a place in his life. It was a nice dream, but in his experience dreams didn't come true, and it was all he could do to make it through his reality.

Someone like Ellie deserved more. But he was a man who had nothing to give.

Opening the door quietly, so not to disturb her, Matt stepped into the hall, took one last look at Ellie before he shut the door, then leaned against the wall for a moment, watching the hotel maid making her way slowly down the corridor with her cart. By the time she reached this room, he'd be on a plane to Hawaii, and from there a military transport back to Iraq.

CHAPTER ONE

"I DON'T KNOW what to do with him," Matt McClain said, looking down at the little tow-headed boy in the firm grasp of his second cousin, or half-cousin, or whatever it was that related them distantly.

Sarah Clayton held the boy's hand like she was holding on to a dog that was about to get away. Tight, and with a purpose. But not friendly. There was nothing friendly *or* nurturing in her. Nothing compassionate. Nothing to indicate she cared at all for the kid. "The same thing you think *I'm* supposed to do with him. Only I'm not going to do it. I took care of your sister those last two weeks, and I've had him with me ever since. But you're here, and you're more blood to him than I am so, he's yours. Besides…"

She held out an envelope—one that had been sealed, opened then sealed again. "Janice left you this."

He opened it, and looked down at the shaky handwriting—the handwriting of a dying woman. A lump formed in his throat and he turned his back to Sarah as he read it.

Dear Matt,
If you're reading this, that means the cancer has
finally beaten me. The doctors said I was too late

for treatment, but that's been my life. Too late for everything. It's called non-Hodgkin's lymphoma, and I'm sure you know all about it since you're a doctor.

Yes, I know you're a doctor. Heard it from a man in the casino where I was working. He was drunk and saying all kinds of crazy things...things that didn't make sense. His name was Carter, I think, and he said he was a doctor. I don't know if that's true, but he was going on about his buddy Matt, from Forgeburn, who saved his life. Great doctor, he called you. And I'm sure you are.

Matt stopped reading for a moment and took a breath. Carter Holmes had been his best buddy since med-school days. He'd sustained almost fatal injuries and, yes, he'd saved his life. "Do you know how long Janice was in Vegas?" he asked Sarah, without turning to face her.

"For a while, I think. She told me she moved around a lot. Changed her name so your old man wouldn't find her. Said she was always looking over her shoulder to make sure he wasn't coming after her."

Matt clenched his jaw, not wanting to read any more but knowing he had to.

I don't blame you for not sending for me, Matty. We were both kids. Neither of us knew what to do. But I did wait until I couldn't stay there anymore. You were gone, Dad left me behind, and even though I wasn't even fifteen I knew I had to leave there, too.

I spent a lot of time going from place to place, never settling down. I was afraid to. Afraid I'd

*get too comfortable someplace and let my guard
down. So I always moved on. Funny thing is, all
those years I was running I guess Dad had died
right after he left Forgeburn. At least that's what
Sarah said. Guess neither of us had to run away,
did we?*

Matt turned to Sarah. "He's dead?"

She nodded. "They found him in one of the canyons.
They think he'd passed on quite a while before one of
the cowboys stumbled on him. He was living like he
always did, they said. Hoarding trash and drinking his
life away. Folks around here said it was the drink that
took him. Didn't really care to find out."

Matt shut his eyes. So many wasted years he and
Janice had had when they could have stayed together.
But they'd become two kids out on their own, in a world
they didn't know. He'd found his salvation in the army.
But Janice... Matt turned away from Sarah again, be-
fore she could see the tears brimming in his eyes.

*I did one good thing, though, Matty. His name
is Lucas. I don't know who his father is, and
there's no sense looking. But he's a good boy—
the only thing I've done right. I want you to take
care of him for me. Make sure he has better than
what we did.*

Do for him, Matty, what you couldn't do for me.

That was where the letter ended. No last words, no
signature. "Is this all?" he asked Sarah.

"It was all she could do to get that on paper. She went
to sleep with the pen still in her hand and she didn't..."

Matt nodded as he looked across the sandy expanse at his sister's grave. A few mourners were still there— maybe five or six and he wondered who they were and why they had come. Forgeburn had never been a real home to them. All it had ever been was the place from which they wanted to escape. "Why did she come back here?" he asked.

"Because she wanted to contact you, but she wasn't up to it. And I was the only relative, even though I live a good fifty miles from here."

"So, Lucas," Matt said, once he'd regained his composure and turned around again to face Sarah. "You've got kids. You know how to take care of them. I don't. And I'm still on active duty. I have to report back in two months." He'd been granted emergency family leave to come and make arrangements for Lucas, but those arrangements didn't include keeping him. That thought had never crossed his mind as he'd assumed Lucas was already settled in with Sarah. But apparently not. "And I'm scheduled to go back to Iraq later this year. How, in all of that, does he fit in?"

"Look, Matt. I kept him until you got here, just to be nice, but this is where it ends. Janice named you as his legal guardian, the social worker from child services has seen to the legalities of it, which makes him your responsibility, not mine. So adopt him yourself, or find someone else who wants him—it's your decision. And I don't mean to be unreasonable about this, but my husband doesn't want him. We've got enough to handle without adding another child to it. So…" She shrugged. "Take him. Or get rid of him. Either way, I'm out of it."

Take him. Just like that. Take a nephew he hadn't even known he had until he'd received word his sister had died.

Matt wasn't opposed to family responsibility. In a lot of ways, he liked the idea of honoring the obligation, even in a family like his. A mother who had left when he'd been five. A sister who had—well, ended up back where she'd started. A dad who apparently had died without notice.

But Lucas—he needed his chance. He hadn't asked to be born into the McClain family. It's just what he'd got. Still, kids didn't belong in his life. He'd planned it like that. No kids, no obligations. *Obligations*—for a moment the image of Ellie flashed through his mind. If ever there'd been a time when he'd come close to taking on an obligation other than his career…

"Look, Sarah, give me a couple weeks to figure it out. Can you do that much?"

Sarah shook her head. "Sorry."

Well, she wasn't giving him many options. For a career military surgeon, always going in one direction or another, moving from place to place and in his case combat zone to combat zone, there was no room to care for a child. In fact, he didn't even have a place to call home, and kids needed a home, and stability. They needed someone there all the time to raise them. They needed what he and Janice had never had.

"All I can say, Matt, is I know you've been doing good for yourself, despite the way your daddy treated you. I'm glad for you. But I can't take Lucas. So, like I said, I've already contacted child services, they know the situation, and the paperwork's started. So he'll go to a group home until they can find a family who'll take him in, unless you do. As for adoption…" She shrugged. "Can't say what'll happen there. He's a cute kid. Doesn't talk, though. Not a word." She leaned in and whispered, "Don't think he's very smart."

"Probably because he's traumatized from everything that's been happening to him," Matt snapped. Then he looked down at Lucas, who was sucking his thumb. He had a ratty old blanket tucked under his arm, and he wore a pair of sneakers that were clearly several sizes too large. All Matt could think was he was so vulnerable. And scared. Matt knew what it was like to be vulnerable and scared. Knew exactly what the kid was feeling…like his whole world had just collapsed. Matt couldn't blame Lucas for not wanting to talk. There had been many times in his own young life when he hadn't wanted to talk either.

"Hope it doesn't mess up your life too much, Matt," Sarah said, then turned and walked away, leaving Matt standing alone in the cemetery, holding on to Lucas with one hand and a bag of clothes with the other. And with no idea what to do next.

"Do you eat hamburgers?" he asked Lucas, who looked up at him with wide, frightened eyes. The kid needed more than a hamburger. Matt knew that. He needed words of reassurance. The promise of a home. A hug. Right now, though, he was equipped to buy him a hamburger. That's all.

Did kids his age eat hamburgers? Matt's medical training told him yes. But his parenting training—well, there was none of that to draw on. No kids in his life, no kids in his future. No home. No wife. He thought back to that morning when he'd left Ellie sleeping and walked away. Too bad he couldn't go back and stay there. It had been nice. No worries. No past. No future. Just that moment in time. Unlike this moment in time, when his only goal was a hamburger, or anything else a two-year-old would eat.

* * *

"I need to do what?" Ellie Landers looked at the ultrasound, and didn't see anything particularly distressing. She knew how to interpret what she was seeing. Her brief time in nursing had taught her that much. And what she saw right now looked perfectly normal.

"Rest more. Eat better. Reduce stress. Cut back on work. You know, the simple things."

She did know, but she wasn't sure why all this applied to her. Dr. Shaffer had just told her the baby was healthy. She was healthy, too. So why the precautions? "But there's nothing wrong with me. You said so just a few minutes ago." Now she was worried.

"Your blood pressure is on the high end of normal. You're at risk for gestational diabetes partly because of your age and partly because your mother has diabetes. And you're chronically tired."

"Because I work eighteen hours a day." Ellie liked Doc Shaffer. He'd been her mother's obstetrician, now he was hers. Medically, he had a great reputation. Personally, he was just plain kind. He'd never asked her to explain the pregnancy. Not that there was much to explain about a two-night fling at a medical conference. All that, plus he had a great heart for his patients and treated them with respect and dignity no matter what the situation. As someone in the medical field, Ellie appreciated that. As a patient, she was glad to have it.

"Cut it back," he said, leaning forward across his desk, looking over at her across the top of his glasses. "You're thirty-four, Ellie. You live a busy life and drive yourself harder than anybody I've ever seen, except your mom. And I don't want you having complications with this pregnancy."

Thirty-four and owner of one of the fastest-growing medical illustration companies in the world. Something she'd built from the ground up. "But you think I could be at risk?"

"You could be, if you don't slow down—which puts your baby at risk."

Her baby. It was strange hearing that, because Ellie had never really thought of this life she was carrying as *her* baby. It was a baby, possibly someone else's baby, depending on whether or not her fling wanted to be a daddy. But *her* baby? Hearing that gave her a maternal jolt she hadn't expected. It wasn't enough to make her change her mind to become a single mom, but it did make Ellie more aware of the baby she was carrying.

"Look, I'll cut back on the hours. Eat better. But I'm not going to go home, kick my feet up and watch old movies for the next almost five months. I have to work. My company needs me, and I need it."

"You're just like your mother. Do you know that?" Doc Shaffer leaned back in his chair, typed something into his computer, then shook his head. "She was as driven as you are. And as stubborn."

Ellie Landers wanted to smile at the comparison, but she couldn't as she didn't want to be like her mother and didn't want to be compared to her either. "And look how successful she's been. She owns one of the largest technology companies in Nevada." And she'd raised a child as a single mom. Well, mostly in absentia. But she did get the credit for hiring the right people to take care of her. All this was something Ellie wasn't prepared to do.

Children needed a real family, a parent or parents who didn't hire someone to take their child to the playground, who didn't pay for the most qualified caregivers but, instead, took responsibility for that care themselves. Family dinners, stories at bedtime. That's what children needed—what Ellie had never had, and what she wasn't able to give. Not with her job or her chosen lifestyle. That's what Ellie had learned from her own upbringing and what she carried with her every day of her life. That kind of life wasn't meant to be her kind of life.

Still, the dream of it—home, family. Husband. It was nice. But so ethereal it made Ellie sad. So that's where she stopped because the rest of the dream was so vague. But the husband was not. Since Reno, she'd had a vision of him. Even more now that she was carrying his baby.

"Whatever the case, stop at Reception on your way out and schedule your next appointment. I'd like to see you back in six weeks as a precautionary measure. Also, I've written you a prescription for prenatal vitamins, and the name of a good physical therapist should your back spasms continue."

"I don't need a therapist for backache and I already take vitamins. I started the day I found out I was pregnant."

"Which is good. But the ones I'm prescribing have more iron—you're a little anemic, and they also have much more folic acid than anything you can get OTC, because you need folic acid. It's for the healthy development of the brain, eyes, cells and nervous system."

"I know," Ellie said. "Remember, I worked in obstetrics?" She'd been a good nurse, but nursing hadn't suited her the way she'd hoped it would. Maybe because it required nurturing in abundance, and she didn't have a speck of it in her. She had been good at the procedural aspects, but had lacked the genuine human touch that was also needed. Ellie could see her shortcoming, and she'd honestly worked to correct it because she loved medicine, but there had always been something missing. She couldn't define it, couldn't describe it to her supervisor when she'd resigned from her job.

And now, ten years later, she still couldn't define what that lack was other than she simply didn't have a nurturer's instinct. But she'd found her niche—medical illustration.

Ellie had always loved drawing and was pretty good at it. Had won a few childhood awards. Turned it into her minor course of study in college. So when she'd read that it was an expanding field with growth potential, she'd jumped at the chance to be part of it, anxious to combine her love of medicine with her love of drawing. Of course, more education had been required. Two additional years of study on top of the four she'd had in nursing school. In those two years, however, she'd gone from not only wanting to be an illustrator but wanting to build her own company. And it was also exciting. Even now, she had no regrets.

"Yes, I know you were a nurse—for about a minute—then you moved on. *Remember that?*"

"And those charts of fetal development you have hanging on the wall in your waiting room..." She smiled. She'd done them. And she'd illustrated numerous medical texts. Plus, they were doing medical videography now.

Doc Shaffer laughed. "Point taken. You've made a name for yourself, but that name must cut back on her hours, and get more rest. You work too hard, Ellie, and while I'm an advocate for women getting on with their lives when they're pregnant, your life is a little over the top. In other words, baby needs some rest."

Rest—that she would do. Even though she wasn't going to keep this baby, she did want to give it every advantage she could coming into this world, and keeping herself healthy was the start of it. "So, is that all you want? Or would you like another pint of blood?"

Doc Shaffer chuckled. "You know what I want, and at the rate you're going, that's a big order."

"Then I'll do better," she promised. And she would. While Ellie didn't want the responsibility of raising a child, not with her fear of turning out to be the kind of mother hers was, she certainly didn't want to put this baby at risk. She'd made her choice the day her dipstick had gone from blue to pink, and nothing had changed since then. She'd tell Dr. Matt McClain he was going to be a father and give him the option to raise their baby. Or she would opt for adoption, if he didn't want to. It was all straightforward. Ellie owned a business and that was her life, all she wanted. Real babies, boyfriends and husbands were not needed.

So all Ellie had to do now was tell someone who'd expected a couple of casual days of fun at a medical convention that casual had turned into commitment. *If that's what he wanted.* He'd seemed like a nice guy. A little distracted. But kind. And polite. Really good looking…traditionally tall, dark and handsome, and rugged. Dark eyes, wavy black hair, rugged. Built like she'd never seen another man built.

Just thinking about him now gave Ellie goosebumps. The way he'd looked those couple of nights when she'd let go of her self-made business-first rules, let her hair down and lived in a fantasy that had never happened in her reality was still with her. He'd hung on in her mind long after Reno. From time to time she'd even caught herself distracted by a daydream of him. A leftover feeling she couldn't explain and didn't want to explore. Then the reality of those days had crept in, about six weeks later.

And now, well—all Ellie had to do was the figurative baby-in-a-basket-on-the-doorstep thing, and hope he'd take that basket in. It was his baby too and not only did he have the right to know, he had the right to be a daddy, if that's what he wanted. Or be involved in the adoption process, if *that's* what he wanted. Either way, she'd know what was going to happen soon. Ellie was glad he was out of the military now and back home, because from here she was headed straight to Forgeburn, Utah.

"It's not a traditional medical practice," Dr. Donald Granger explained. "But you know that since you're from here. Most of it's a cowboy practice now, and that's about as tough as it gets. Then you've got some of the canyon resort areas with tourists who need medical care occasionally. And we do have some locals in a couple little spread-out towns. There's a pretty fair patient base—enough to keep one doc busy.

"If you need help, the clinic in Whipple Creek will usually send someone out for a day or two, but you've got to keep in mind that you're the only real medical help within a hundred miles in any direction. So what you'll be getting is a practice that stretches out for more miles than any practical medical practice should have to, house calls that'll take up half your day for something minor—and, yes, house calls are part of what the people here expect—and the cowboy trailers—good luck finding those.

"It's a hard life, son. But a good one. People will appreciate you more because access to you isn't easy for many of them. And there's no one to rely on but you, which develops stamina. And courage. Lots of courage."

"If it's so good," Matt asked, "why are you giving it up?" He had qualms about taking over a GP practice, even if only for a little while because being back home came with all kinds of bad memories, and he was afraid those might surface at the wrong times and prevent him from doing his best. Plus, he wasn't a GP. That was another big drawback. In fact, the only good thing was that it would keep him busy, and he needed that. Lucas was a great kid, but spending every minute of every day together wasn't good for either of them. They both needed some separation from time to time.

"I've been doing it for fifty years, as you know, since I took care of you when you were little. And these old bones aren't rugged enough anymore. Also, I've got grandkids who don't even know me. So it's time for me to move on, to rest the weary bones and play with the grandkids."

"You do realize I'm only going to be a temp here. Once the situation with Lucas gets straightened out, I have to report back to duty. They've given me two months, which is the time I've accrued for regular leave. So you'll still have to keep looking for someone to buy you out."

"Or close the practice for good if I can't." Dr. Granger held out his hands. They were knotted with arthritis. "These hands can't do the job anymore, Matt, or I would carry on. I wouldn't want to see this place go without a doctor, but most of the young docs coming out of medical school want something better than what I've got to offer, and the older docs who have had something better now want something simpler. Practicing in Forgeburn doesn't just take love for the work, it takes love for the work *here*."

That would never happen. Once child services had a good placement for Lucas, he'd be gone. Being here was only a matter of circumstances, and Matt wasn't staying because he wanted to. He was staying for Lucas. "So, when do you want me to start?"

"Are you sure about this, Matt? Do you really want to do this?"

"No. But, I'm not staying here for me. The army has me and I'll go back as soon as I can."

"And that little one you're looking after?"

"Lucas is a good kid, and I'm going to make sure I've found the best situation for him before I leave. If that means staying here for longer than I'd wanted, that's what I'll do because I don't want him growing up the way I did. You know how it was with Janice and me, Doc—and no kid deserves that."

"But you came through it, Matt, and look at you now."

Yes, just look at him. The man who knew nothing about kids as temporary guardian of a child he couldn't raise. Kids needed much more than anything he had to offer. In fact, as it stood, Matt had nothing to offer whatsoever. His life in the army didn't mix with domesticity in any form. "But my sister didn't, which is why I have to do what I'm doing. I owe it to her to do this for Lucas." Even though he was sure Janice's intention had been for him to keep the boy. But that wouldn't work out.

"Well, OK, then. How about starting right now? Oh, and talk to Betty Nelson about watching Lucas. She's a retired teacher. Really good with little ones. I couldn't recommend anyone better than her."

"I'll do that," Matt said, thinking back to his grade-school days. Betty Nelson had been his teacher for a year. She'd paid for his lunch, and Janice's, when he hadn't had money—which had been pretty much every day. And she'd made sure that he'd had his school supplies even though his dad had refused to pay for them. She'd be a perfect babysitter for Lucas, and Matt was keeping his fingers crossed she would do that. "I'll definitely talk to her."

So now this was where he put on his stethoscope and stepped into a completely different life. For a little while. That's what he'd keep telling himself—for a little while.

But what if he couldn't find a good situation for Lucas? Could he walk away from him knowing he was leaving Lucas where he, himself, had been left so many times during his own childhood?

No, he didn't want to think about that. Didn't want to think into the future. Reality, here and now, was good enough. Always had been because it's all he'd ever been able to count on. Getting by, moment to moment.

Sighing, Matt held out his hand for the keys to the clinic. This was for Janice, he reminded himself. For Janice and Lucas. It didn't make things easier, but it made him feel better. It's what he had to do—that's the thought that ran through his mind for the next few hours as he prepared himself mentally to be part of Forgeburn again.

The clinic was small, just as he remembered it. One underwhelming exam room with basic outdated equipment, a minor procedures room, a shared public and staff bathroom, a small reception area and waiting room, which seated only six people, and a tiny, knee-hole office. But it did have a nice storage room attached to his office, larger than he would have expected, with a window at the rear of it overlooking a rock formation in the distance.

A playroom for Lucas when Betty Nelson couldn't watch him? Switch to a Dutch door for security, add carpeting—it was a thought. One that didn't go away as he walked around the outside of the small white cement building that stood alone in the middle of a cracked asphalt parking lot, surrounded by sand, dirt and a lot of cacti.

The next closest structure, a small, nineteen-sixties-style hotel was, with a lot of squinting, within eyesight. There really was no upside to the medical office, nothing nice or pretty or comforting, but the house he'd also be getting as part of the deal was definitely an upside. Modestly large, fairly new, with a nice pool and beautiful canyon view. A squared-off adobe-style with an open floor plan, large kitchen—he used to love to cook—and a *casita* with in-home or private access. Not that he needed a *casita*, since he didn't anticipate anyone ever coming to visit him. But at least it gave him an option.

"This is where we'll be staying," he said to Lucas the next day as they explored the outside area together, to make sure the pool was completely secured and safe, grateful Doc Granger's one indulgence in life had been his house. It would be a good place for Lucas. Comfortable. Safe. "How about we go take a look?" He'd wanted to carry Lucas, but Lucas was often resistant to that, unless he was tired. *A child with determination*, Matt thought.

Lucas's reaction was to turn his back to Matt and

stare at a little brown and blue skink darting into a rock garden at the edge of the patio. It was trying to get away from prying eyes. Sort of what Matt felt like doing, to be honest. "Well, if you're not interested in looking around today, we'll be back tomorrow when we move in. Plenty of time for exploring then."

Especially since Doc Granger had already vacated the place. Except for the furniture, which was staying with the house, all the personal touches were gone. And Matt had an idea Doc Granger was, right now, playing with grandkids. Which meant Matt was totally on his own here. It wasn't an unsettling thought, but it wasn't a comforting one either, since he knew so little about his new responsibilities. Well, live and learn. He'd make the best of it, like he was making the best of being a temporary dad.

"You ready to leave?" he finally asked Lucas, who'd gone over to the rocks, looking for the skink. Of course, Lucas didn't answer. Neither did he take Matt's hand when Matt extended it to him. Instead, he took an extra-firm hold on the ratty old blanket he carried with him everywhere, and trailed along next to Matt. Never too close, but never too far.

There were two cars in the parking lot. Actually, one car and a pick-up truck. And there was little to indicate this was a medical clinic except the weather-beaten sign at the edge of the parking lot that read: "Medical Clinic". Followed by an emergency phone number.

"Well, this is it," Ellie said. It had become her habit to talk to her baby. While she was only just past eighteen weeks along, and babies in the womb didn't start hearing until around twenty-three weeks, she liked the connection. Felt that, on some level, it would help her baby's development. So she talked.

"Not what I expected. For some reason, I'd guessed your daddy to be...better established." Of course, they'd never really talked about such things. They'd talked about other things, especially that first night—medicine, college days, the convention—but never about their own realities. That had been part of keeping it from becoming too personal. Of course, that hadn't worked out, had it?

Ellie glanced down at her belly as she stepped out of her car. It wasn't exactly flat now, but loose-fitting cargo pants and an oversized white, gauzy shirt still concealed the obvious. Not for much longer, though, as her naked profile was that of a woman with a bulging belly. But right now her baggy clothes kept her condition a secret from her co-workers—she didn't want to answer all the questions—and from Matt as well, until she found the right moment to tell him.

What she didn't want was for him to open the door to her and see her belly right off. Why shock him like that? It wouldn't be right.

Also, she wanted to reassure herself he was someone she wanted to raise the baby because Reno hadn't been about real life, whereas this baby definitely was. So Ellie wanted to know, see more, before she let Matt know what had happened. She'd thought about how to handle the inevitable the whole way here, and hadn't come up with a real solution yet. Time would tell, she supposed as she entered the building, only to discover a completely empty waiting room. No patients, no receptionist. Just chairs and a desk.

"Well, it's clean," she whispered, as she wandered

down the short hall leading to the exam room, looking for signs of life. "Anybody here?" she finally called out.

Ellie listened, heard noises coming from the room marked "EXAM" and moved a little closer. "Hello?" she called out again.

This time there was an answer. "There is, and I'll be with you in about five minutes. Please, take a seat in the waiting room."

She recognized the voice, of course. Nice, smooth. Very sexy. A voice worthy of goose-bumps that were, coincidentally, already running up her arms. "Thank you," she called back. It was closer to ten minutes, though, before a young woman, who wore khaki shorts and worn hiking boots, wandered down the hall and out the front door, sporting an elastic brace on her left arm. And it was another couple of minutes before Matt appeared in the waiting room, with a little boy at his side.

"Ellie?" he said, frowning at first then slowly giving a broad smile. "I—I didn't expect to see you here." He took quick steps in her direction, then stopped before the predictable embrace "How have you been?"

She stopped as well, suddenly feeling uncertain about what she was doing here. "I've been fine, Matt. I was vacationing nearby, and thought I would stop by to see you. If you don't mind."

"Mind? Absolutely not. I...um... I'm glad to see you," he said, obviously surprised and a little off kilter.

This was so awkward. She felt it. He felt it. But she was here and now she had to go through with her plan. Well, maybe not this very moment. But in a while. "I'm glad to see you, too. I wasn't sure if you'd want me to look you up, but I took a chance and..." Ellie took two more steps in Matt's direction, but too quickly as her head started spinning, spinning as the hallway slowly descended into darkness. Her last words before she toppled into his arms were, "My baby..."

CHAPTER TWO

NOTHING SEEMED ABNORMAL. Ellie's blood pressure was a little high, but not outside normal. Her pulse was fine. So were her reflexes and her heartbeat. She'd come to before he'd had a chance to do anything more than a cursory exam and had stopped him.

Right now, she was sitting up, sipping water. Fully alert. Offering no explanation for anything. And he didn't buy that she was here vacationing. She wasn't the type to vacation. Maybe travel for work but not for pleasure. Especially to a place like this. So, did she want to take what they'd started to the next level, even though they'd agreed to keep it casual?

The thought of that caused Matt's heart to skip a beat, even though he wasn't a next-level kind of guy. The idea of it did intrigue him, though, because he'd had that thought a time or two, then dismissed it as impractical. It couldn't work. They lived in different worlds. But it had been a nice thought for those few moments.

"You mentioned something about a baby, so I checked your car and..." He shrugged. "No baby."

"I call my car my baby," Ellie said, not looking at him.

He didn't buy that either. But he wasn't going to pressure her into telling him what she wanted because Ellie was direct. She'd do it in her own good time. "Well, your car's fine."

She didn't respond. Just nodded and kept on sipping.

"So, you said you're vacationing here?"

Ellie nodded again.

"In Forgeburn, where the population is in negative numbers?" This was getting more and more interesting, and he couldn't wait until she told him the truth. Which she would because Ellie wasn't a very good liar. It was showing on her face and in her fidgety hands. Normally, she was straightforward. At least, she had been in Reno. Yet this side of Ellie—it didn't fit what he knew of her. Which really wasn't much, come to think of it.

"You said the scenery here was beautiful, so I decided to check it out for myself."

"During the off-season when the resorts aren't operating at full capacity? Funny, I would have taken you for someone who'd want all the amenities."

"Is the little boy yours? Because he looks exactly like you," she said, obviously trying to avoid what she'd come here to say—or do. "I don't remember you saying anything about having a child. Or a wife. Do you have a wife, too?"

Was she really here to see him again? The thought crossed his mind but didn't stay there. Because Ellie had vehemently denied wanting a relationship. Which he'd been glad about. So why now, when he was on leave, had she turned up? And how did she even know he was on leave? Or where he'd be? "I've never married. And Lucas… He's my nephew, and I'm temporarily his legal guardian."

"Nephew?"

"My sister died, which left her son in my care, temporarily."

"Why not permanently?"

"I'm in the army. Single. Get transferred a lot because I'm a surgeon who likes to see action, as in battlefield. It's not a great combination for raising a kid as a single dad."

"You haven't retired?" Ellie asked, looking puzzled.

"No. I'm going back as soon as I fix the situation with Lucas. Hopefully, that'll be inside two months. So, how did you find me? How did you know I was in Forgeburn?"

"Part of my job is research. You were easy to track once I got to the right department in the army, and they connected me to your superior officer, who was very helpful."

It wasn't that simple for most people, and for a moment Matt admired her ability to not only find his superior officer but get him to tell her just where, on leave, he was. "But they neglected to tell you I was coming back?"

"They probably figured you'd tell me when I caught up to you."

"Well, you've caught up to me, and I'm wondering why."

"Like I said, a vacation. Oh, and I'm so sorry about your sister. It can't have been easy on you or Lucas."

"It hasn't been, and I appreciate your sympathy for my sister. She was a good sort who never really got a break in life." What was Ellie up to? It bothered Matt, not knowing. But what bothered him even more was how glad he was to see her.

* * *

This wasn't at all what she'd expected, and she wasn't sure which way to go with it, especially since Matt had made up his mind about what he was going to do. Get rid of Lucas then go back to the army. Which meant everything she'd hoped for when she had been told he'd gone home was up in the air. Ellie had assumed he was out of the army. He wasn't. And she'd hoped he would be settled enough to want their baby. Again, he wasn't. Also, he didn't even want Lucas.

So where did that leave her? Basically, at square one again. Pregnant without a plan. Except she would tell him and still give him the opportunity to raise his child. That was only fair. "Well, I need a room. The hotel down the road is a little…dated. Is there someplace better?"

Matt chuckled. "Like I said, the best places aren't running at full capacity yet, and the rest of the smaller places—I'm not sure you'd like them. Especially since I know, for a fact, you prefer satin sheets."

Satin sheets. Yes, she'd loved the feel of them, and the feel of him next to her as she'd enjoyed the soft caress of both the sheets and Matt. "I'm not really concerned about sheets, Matt. I just need some food, then bed…" For her pregnancy first, but also for her because she was tired. She needed to put her feet up, close her eyes and give both her and the baby at least ten hours of down time. Maybe more, if she could.

"If you go down the road, about five miles in the opposite direction, there's a place called Red Canyon Resort. It has nice rooms, decent amenities. Since it's early in the season, you shouldn't have trouble getting a room. But if you *do* stay…"

He stopped, paused for a moment, and that hesitation of a frown she'd seen on his face when he'd first seen her a little while ago returned. Only this time it didn't transform into a smile. She hoped he was glad to see her. In fact, she'd thought he was. Now she wasn't so sure.

"If you do stay, there's not much to do unless you like hiking or rock climbing," he finally continued.

"I'll manage," she said, scooting to the edge of the exam table, feeling a little more discouraged than she had before. Of course, she'd never been totally optimistic about asking him. That would have been foolish, given the circumstances. But she'd hoped. Right now, though, some of the hope was disappearing— because of Lucas, because of Matt's military commitments, because he was more rigid than she remembered him being.

"Before you go, I'd really like to get a better look at you. Something caused you to faint, and I don't know what it was."

"I was tired from the drive. Hungry. Probably a little dehydrated. Once I get a room, I'll eat, drink plenty of fluids, get some rest, and I'll be fine." Ellie scooted a little more until she was at the edge, then stretched until her feet were on the floor. As soon as she stood, though, she wobbled, and Matt was right there to catch her. Again.

"I think before you go checking into anywhere, I'm going to take you someplace to get something to eat. And drink. Your skin doesn't pass the pinch test, so I think your biggest problem right now is dehydration. Are you diabetic, by any chance?"

"Nope. Just had a physical yesterday, as it turns out. Blood tests were good."

"No kidney disease?"

"I'm fine, Matt. My doctor told me I needed to get some rest, which is why I'm here."

"You live in Reno. You could have driven an hour over to Tahoe and checked into a world-class resort to rest there, instead of driving six hundred miles through the desert to rest here. If rest is what you're really after."

"Right now, it is. I don't suppose there'd be a cab out here I could call. I don't think I'm going to be able to drive."

He doubted she'd even make it to her car. "Look, Lucas and I were headed home when you came in. How about you go with us, I'll make sure you get plenty of liquids, and I'll fix us a good dinner? Then later we'll see if you're in any condition to check into a hotel."

Matt took Ellie by the arm and steadied her to the floor again, but instead of letting her attempt to walk to his truck he swooped her into his arms and carried her like he had that first morning, when she had been looking out the window and he had been looking at her—with a longing that hadn't been quenched. He'd swooped her into his arms then, and had watched the satin sheet slither to the floor as he'd laid her naked body down on the bed, and laid his naked body over hers. Thinking about that, even now, caused her to shiver.

"This is very chivalrous of you," she said, without protest. Ellie still liked being in his arms, still liked the feel of him pressed to her. Matt had the power to knock her completely off track, and she couldn't let that happen. Couldn't let the thoughts of how good they had been together seep in. Couldn't let the thoughts of how nice it was to be in his arms, yet again, seep in either.

"I aim to give the best medical care I can, under the circumstances." Matt looked over at Lucas, who was occupied with a toddler version of a video game. "You ready to go home?" he asked.

Lucas picked up his video toy and his blanket, and went directly to Matt's side, the way he always did. Then fell into exact step with Matt, the way he'd only just started doing. "He doesn't talk yet," he explained to Ellie as they walked through the parking lot. "He's lived in some pretty rough circumstances for a while and he's a little delayed, but he's bright. Understands everything. Very observant of everything around him. Just not talkative.

"He will, when he has something to say. Guess he just hasn't had anything to say yet." She wiggled into the passenger's seat, while Matt strapped Lucas into the toddler safety seat in the crew cab, and within a minute they were on their way to what Matt had dubbed Matt Casa. She still wasn't sure what to make of any of this, but one thing was certain—she did like the way he took care of Lucas. Liked it very much. And the way he took care of her went far, far beyond like.

What had she been thinking, taking that ten-hour drive in one long stretch, stopping only a few times for breaks? Well, a little rest, a little water, a good bed under her back for the night, and she'd be fine. But this sure wasn't the way she'd wanted her first meeting with Matt to go. Seriously, fainting into his arms? Ellie doubted she could have made a more dramatic entrance if she'd tried.

Anyway, telling him about the baby would keep until

tomorrow, when she was rested. Yep, back to the plan, but only a modified version of it since she already knew Matt's intentions. No Lucas, no family commitments. But would that include his own child as well? Maybe something about bringing his own child into the world would mellow him, or cause him to change his mind. Ellie wasn't counting on it, though. But she wasn't ruling it out either.

Right now, though, she was going home with Matt. Not part of the plan but so far nothing else had been either. "Since you're obviously not working as a surgeon out here, what kind of practice do you run?"

"Well, I suppose you could call it a family practice or a general practice. The doc who had it before me called it a cowboy practice, and I think that works. Bottom line, I'll get to treat everything as long as I'm here."

As long as he was here. Suddenly, Ellie felt discouraged and disappointed. She'd wanted him to want their baby—it would have been the perfect solution. But there was no solution now. At least, not one she could think of. The thought of that brought tears to her eyes—tears Matt would never see as she turned her head to the window and pretended to be caught up in night-time stars.

"You have two choices. There's a *casita* adjoining the house and it has everything you'll need if you want to sleep there tonight. Or you can stay in one of the guest bedrooms. Your choice."

"How about the *casita*, since I don't feel like climbing stairs? My legs are a little stiff from the drive. Back's a little achy, too."

"Does your doctor know what you did?" Matt asked, leading Ellie through the hall to the entry to the *casita*—a nice little one-bedroom house with a small kitchen and a reasonably large living area. Traditionally, a *casita* was used by a family member or long-term guest. Or tonight, his two-night fling in Reno.

That was an odd question—out of the blue asking her doctor's opinion. Did Matt suspect she was pregnant? Quickly, she looked to make sure her belly hadn't puffed out a few inches and she hadn't noticed. But that wasn't the case. Underneath her baggy cotton shirt, it showed. But not with the shirt on. Whatever the case, she approached her answers cautiously because she was too tired and discouraged to address anything other than sleep tonight.

"No. I really don't have to account to anybody for anything in my life, and that includes my doctor. And before you ask, he would have advised against the drive until I was on vitamins with iron for a few days. Low-grade anemia. Nothing serious. But, like I said, I make my own decisions, and I decided to come to Forgeburn for a holiday."

"As you've said," Matt stated. He opened the door to the *casita* then stepped aside. "Well, whatever the case, it should take me about an hour to fix something to eat, so in the meantime I'd suggest you rest. There's a nice patio outside, and there's the bedroom…your choice."

"You really don't have to do this, Matt. I'm used to taking care of myself. The Red Canyon Resort would be fine."

"You look run-down. I wouldn't call that taking care of yourself."

"I work hard. Travel a lot. My business is growing, and I've got some amazing opportunities coming up. Also, like I said, it's low-grade anemia. All that earns me the right to look run-down. But a good night's sleep will work wonders."

He knew better, though, because he was beginning to suspect. "Well, then, dinner's in an hour. And I don't remember. Are you a vegetarian? I seem to recall you might be."

"I am," she said. "Hope that doesn't put you to any trouble."

"Nope. Because all I have here are chicken nuggets and hot dogs, neither of which are very good."

"Not healthy for Lucas either. Or you, for that matter." With that, she entered the *casita* and shut the door behind her, leaving Matt to stand in the hall staring at—nothing. He was staring at nothing. Until a tug on his shirt tail reminded him that Lucas needed to be fed, bathed and put to bed before anything else happened.

Matt sighed as he sat on the veranda, looking up at the stars. It was a beautiful night. Clear. And the view from this house was stunning. Growing up here, he'd never thought anything about the area was stunning. Not the scenery, the people, the wildlife. Especially not the cramped, rundown house trailers he'd grown up in, where his dad had got the bed, his sister the sofa, and he had been welcome to any spot he could find on the floor that wasn't cluttered with some sort of rubbish. Trailers in a rubbish lot, parked and ready to go for scrap.

He'd escaped that when he'd been sixteen. Had run away to Las Vegas, promising Janice he'd send for her as soon as he could. Well, that had never happened and now all he had left were bad memories of bad times, and a little boy who served to remind him of how he'd broken his promise to Janice. It wasn't a very good legacy, but he'd been able to put some of it aside in the army. Or, at least, justify it to himself. Too young. Too inexperienced in the world. Yeah, whatever.

And his promise to himself about never coming back to Forgeburn for any reason—fat lot of good that had done him because here he was. Maybe he deserved to be here, if only to remind him of what he could have become. Or what Janice could have become if he'd kept his promise. "Care for a margarita?" he asked Ellie, who sat down at a patio table across from him.

"I don't drink," she said. "Water's good, though."

"I seem to recall a couple of mojitos in Reno. But if you don't drink now…" He shrugged. "Water, vegetarian—that sounds like a mighty healthy lifestyle."

"We all make our choices, I suppose. My mom's diabetic and my dad, well, I never knew him because he was a number in a sperm catalogue. Someone with the right qualities to produce a good baby."

"That's what your mother told you?"

"We Landers women are very—forthcoming."

"And it doesn't bother you, knowing you were…"

"You can say it. I was the product of my mother's egg and her donor of choice. Now, about that water…"

He was stunned by how casually she took her parentage. It was simply a matter of fact, move on. He didn't know whether to admire it or pity it. "Well, I did find a few healthy things in the fridge and put a couple of salads together. Lots of *pico de gallo*, avocado, cilantro, corn, tomatoes—that sort of thing. I didn't add the jalapeños because I wasn't sure you could do spicy."

"I do spicy just fine, as long as it's not *too* spicy."

Matt stood. "Well, let me go get dinner, then."

"Lucas is in bed?" she asked.

"Asleep before his head hit the pillow." He took a few steps toward the veranda door then stopped but didn't turn to face her. "Is it mine?" he asked, quite simply.

"Is *what* yours?"

"The baby. I'm assuming it's mine, or otherwise you wouldn't be here." Matt blew out a long, anxious breath. "You *did* come to tell me I'm going to be a father, didn't you?"

"I did."

He nodded, his composure perfectly intact, then went into the house, leaving Ellie sitting alone outside. Once he got in, however, his passive demeanor gave way and his knees nearly buckled under him. In fact, it was all he could do to make it from the dining area just inside the door to the kitchen, which wasn't more than about twenty steps. And with every step he took he fought to push it out of his mind. Willed himself to not think. Forced himself to pick up the salads, pour Ellie a glass of water and make that long trip back outside to her. Not that he'd be able to eat now. Just the thought of food almost caused him to gag.

"I made some tortillas to go along with the salad," he said, sitting back down, deliberately not looking at her, even though he knew she was staring at him.

"Are you always this cool under pressure?" she asked.

"When you work in a battlefield, you have to be cool."

"But this isn't a battlefield, Matt, and you're not working."

"No, I'm not. But what I *am* doing is trying to figure out where this conversation goes from here. It's a first for me."

"How about something where you're very excited about becoming a dad. Or you're very angry. Either one would be a start."

"But I'm not excited. Not angry either. I'm just… stunned. That's big news and I need some time to let it sink in."

"I'm not here to pressure you," Ellie said. "But I didn't think this kind of news should be dealt with over the phone, which is the real reason I'm here. I came to tell you in person. So, any initial thoughts…reactions?"

He poured himself a glass of margarita, took a long drink, then finally looked at her. "Numb. I'm numb. And shocked. And confused." He took another drink. "So, now it's your turn. Tell me how *you're* feeling."

Ellie actually laughed. "At first, pretty much the same way you are. I didn't plan this, Matt. We used protection. I know you mentioned that the condom had slipped but I wasn't fertile—at least, I shouldn't have been. I mean, having a little fling in a hotel with a stranger isn't me. I've never done that before. Then to have this happen as a result…" She shook her head. "It certainly changes things, doesn't it?"

It did, and he wasn't anywhere close to being ready to think about them. First things first. He had to come to terms with a baby—*his* baby—coming into this world in what he estimated to be about another twenty-three weeks, give or take. "So, should I ask the obvious? Are you sure it's mine?"

"You were the first man I'd been involved with in over four years, and there's been nobody since. But, if you need proof, we could have tests…"

This discussion was too rigid. It was as if they were talking about something impersonal, like what kind of tongue depressors to order. But damn. Matt didn't know the etiquette or protocol for this kind of situation, if there was such a thing. "No. I don't need proof." He trusted her. Even though he didn't know Ellie that well, something about her made Matt trust her. Maybe because she was—different. Very honest, very open. He'd found that an attractive quality when he'd met her in Reno.

This is what it is, Matt. No strings. Only a diversion for a night. Can you handle that?

It was especially attractive as no one in his life had ever been open or honest with him. *Going for a walk*, his old man would say. *Be right back*. Except right back often turned into two or three weeks. *There'll be food on the table tonight, son. I just got paid*. Except the only thing on the table was an empty booze bottle.

So, yes, he appreciated her honesty. Now more than before. "I believe you. So, what's the bottom line here, Ellie?" It occurred to him he didn't even know her real name. Was Ellie short for Eleanor or Elizabeth or Elena? And did she have a middle name?

"The bottom line is I came to Forgeburn to see if you want to be involved in this. It's your child, too, and you have every right to be a father in any way you want."

"You don't mince words, do you?"

"Like I said about the Landers women... Anyway, I knew after I passed out you'd probably suspect something like this. Especially since we were just a fling. So why bother pretending it's anything other than what it is? We took the first step together in creating this child, I took the second step in coming here to tell you, so now the next step is yours."

"As in financial obligation? Because I don't have a

lot. I'm military, not private sector. But I'll certainly do my part."

"I was thinking something a little more substantial than that."

Matt swallowed hard. Something was coming, and it wasn't going to be good. "Define more substantial."

"Well, I'm not going to raise this baby. I don't want to be a single mom the way my mother and grandmother both were. The women in my family lack maternal instinct, and this baby wasn't in my plan. But I want to make sure he, or she, gets the best possible start in life. After that, I'm going to step aside because my life won't accommodate a child, and I don't want to raise a child the way my mother raised me—with tutors and nannies. Which is what would happen, given my involvements. Children need more than that, more than I had, and I don't have what they need. I'm smart enough to realize that. So, for starters, no abortion. We created this child, and it deserves a chance at life. Even though I'm only eighteen weeks along, I feel...an attachment."

Ellie paused for a moment, and her eyes went distant. Maybe to a place where she was holding the baby or singing it a lullaby. That's where Matt's mind was for that instant. The two of them, huddled together with their baby, looking so happy. But the image disappeared, to be replaced by an image of a battlefield surgery, and the blood, the distant gunshots. "So, if you've ruled out abortion..."

"The reason I'm here is to ask you if you want to raise the baby. Take full custody, let me pay *you* child support, and allow me to step away from it. At least, that was my intention before I knew you were still in the army, so now..."

Matt swallowed hard, again. He knew what was on the other end of that sentence. Because if he didn't, she'd give the child—his child—up for adoption. How was it that just a few simple weeks ago his life was set? He knew where he wanted to be, and what he wanted to be doing. And now he had not one but two children who were both on the verge of being given up. Damn, what was he going to do about that?

CHAPTER THREE

"IT COULD HAVE been worse." Ellie dropped down on her bed and eased out a sigh. She was tired, and she was a little worried that she'd fainted. But Matt was a good doctor, which made her feel better. At least for now. But in the morning?

Sleep didn't come as easily as she'd hoped it would, though. For the first half-hour she tossed and turned, and willed every thought out of her mind. Which didn't work. So she punched the pillow for the fifth or sixth time, and thought about what a nice place this would be to raise a baby. Nice house. Beautiful landscape all around it. And she didn't mind the isolation. In a way it soothed her, held back the pressures.

Another time, another life, this might have been the kind of place she would have chosen for herself. Just the three of them, or actually four. Taking hikes in the desert together. Going for adventures near some of the old Anasazi pueblo ruins she'd seen on the road coming in. Maybe buying a couple of horses and learning to ride. Such an idyllic life, but that wasn't her life. Giving Matt the opportunity to raise the baby then going back to her business was. And it was on that note, the one that was always familiar, Ellie finally went to sleep.

* * *

Who to talk to when there was nobody to talk to? That's what his life boiled down to. Nobody. No old friends here anymore. Anybody Matt would have considered a casual friend was still in the army and somewhere overseas. It was disconcerting, realizing exactly how alone he was, but make no mistake. He was alone here. But, damn, if ever there was a time he needed to talk, it was now.

He thought about Carter Holmes, his old partner back in Kandahar. Top-notch surgeon, maybe even better than Matt, and Matt considered himself pretty damned good. They'd walked the walk for several months, had partnered as well as any two docs could, and had become close—the kind of closeness that could only happen on the battlefield. They'd seen things together, done things together than no person should ever have to see or do. And had come through it.

Except Carter's coming through hadn't been all that great. He'd taken some shrapnel, it had been touch and go with life for a while, and had come out with some PTSD working against him.

Lucky for Carter, he'd had a good woman waiting for him back home. That lucky son of a— And that's where Matt assumed he was now. In her arms, pulling his life back together. Which meant Carter didn't need to hear about Matt's problems. Not now. In a way, he envied Carter what he had, though. It was something he couldn't foresee for himself, but it was…nice. A settled life. Stability. Someone to love who loved him back. Nice dream, but not his dream.

So, once again, nobody to talk to. Normally, it didn't matter. Right now, in the wee hours, it did.

Blowing out a frustrated breath, Matt took a quick look in at Lucas to make sure he was OK, then went outside to the veranda. Sat down, stared up at the moon. Listened to the far-off howl of a wolf. No one howled back at him either.

"Pregnancy requires proper nutrition," Matt said, chopping sweet cubanelle peppers into the skillet.

He looked good. Nice jeans, nice T-shirt. Rugged. But not rested. Her fault, she was sure. Ellie felt bad for that as she hadn't wanted any of this to be disruptive. Of course, what had she expected? *Hi, remember me from a few months back? Well, I'm your baby mama now.*

"And my nutrition is good. Nothing to worry about there," Ellie said, sitting down at the kitchen table, pleased that he was taking care of her. No one ever had unless they had been paid to. This was strange— but nice.

"What does your doctor have to say about that?" Matt asked, turning away from the counter to face her. He wiped his hands on a cloth towel and slung it over his shoulder.

"He's fine with that part of my pregnancy."

"Is there anything you haven't told him yet?" he asked, crossing over to the refrigerator. He pulled out a wire basket of fruit and sat it down. "Because, as your attending physician…"

"He knows what he needs to know," she snapped, then instantly regretted it. Matt didn't need her mood— and, yes, she did have mood swings. That was the worst part of pregnancy so far. But to swing on Matt—he was trying to be the good guy here. The one in the white hat. While she was the stranger who had come riding in to interrupt his life. "Look, I know I'm not supposed to have it, but coffee…"

Matt shook his head. "No caffeine. And while I probably don't have the right to tell you that, remember you're the one who came to me with this…well, it's not a problem. Children aren't problems. But it's a situation. And because half that situation is mine, I do get some say."

She liked the forcefulness. Smooth yet firm. And sexy. Not that a woman in her condition had any business looking at sexy anything. Or did they? Ellie honestly didn't know if those kinds of feelings stirred during pregnancy, and she sure wasn't going to ask Matt, since he was the one stirring them. Maybe she'd ask Doc Shaffer when she got home. Or just ignore everything.

"You do," she conceded. "You're right about the coffee, too. I have moments of weakness, though. Don't give in to them, but sometimes they do surface."

Matt prepped the fruit and dumped it into a juicer, then tidied the kitchen. He said nothing for the next couple of minutes. Not a single word. And Ellie felt awkward, since she'd envisioned long talks with him and forging some sort of bond. But with his back to her, there was nothing to do other than sit and wait until he turned around and either gave her the smoothie or decided to talk. "How do you know I don't have a fruit allergy?" she finally said after the silence just got too much for her.

"Well, first off, since you see me preparing fruit, I'd assume you'd tell me if you did have an allergy. Also, that first night in Reno, when I was ordering late-night room service, you told me you were healthy. Weren't allergic to anything."

"You remembered that?" Ellie was surprised that he had since that was such a small detail in the scheme of everything else that had happened between them. Surprised, but pleased. Did that mean he might have thought about her since then? Or was she reading too much into something that really didn't matter?

"Had to. Didn't want to order something that would result in an EpiPen later. Didn't have one with me either." Matt turned and handed her a tumbler of the fruit drink. Then smiled. "I also remember that you're a left-side-of-the-bed person, almost to the point of an OCD problem."

"It's not that bad," she said, blushing. Was he flirting with her?

"Yes, it is. But it didn't matter because I can adjust to any side of the bed, the floor, a cot, a trench or foxhole..." He shrugged. "And I have, on all of them."

"Because of the army?"

"Because I spent my childhood sleeping on the floor, or anyplace else I could find that wasn't covered with my old man's..." Matt stopped. Turned back to the sink to rinse the blender.

"Your old man's what?" Ellie asked him.

"Rubbish," he said. "My old man's rubbish. He found it on the street, in alleys, in trash bins, and carted it home then dumped it wherever he could. Including the spot on the floor I would have cleared the night before so I could sleep."

"You slept on the floor? In filth?"

"Filth, rodents, bugs." He turned back round to face her. "That's what squatters and beggars do."

Ellie didn't even know what to say to that and judging from the cold expression she saw in his eyes now, she thought it best not go anywhere near it.

"When did you go to the store?" she asked, hoping to change the conversation to something not quite as explosive as his childhood seemed to have been. "Because last night you didn't have any of this." She held up her smoothie.

"This morning, on my way to take Lucas to his babysitter—Betty Nelson."

"Is she good?" Ellie asked. "My mother always went through a lengthy interview process to find my nannies and tutors, but there were a couple of them she hired..." She cringed, thinking about the mistakes her mother had made finding good child care on several occasions, and wondering if she herself would have what was necessary to find the right adoptive parents for the baby. What if she made a mistake, the way her mother had done occasionally? The difference was her mother had fired her mistakes. She, on the other hand, would doom the baby to a lifetime living with the mistake she could make. It was a sobering thought and a frightening one.

"Betty's great. And the best part is she's flexible. I can take Lucas to her any time, day or night. She doesn't mind."

"Then you're lucky."

"I am, but I'd rather keep him with me as much as I can. Probably something to do with not ever having a real parent myself. At least, while Lucas is with me, I can be a real parent."

A temporary parent, she thought. Could Matt not see what would happen when another parent was found for Lucas? It was going to crush that child. Already her heart was breaking for that little boy. But it wasn't her place to say anything, so she didn't. "Well, sometimes having a real parent isn't all that it's cracked up to be. I did, and it didn't work out so well for me. Anyway, I think I'll take this smoothie with me—which is delicious, by the way—go take a shower, then maybe we'll have time to really talk about what we're going to do."

"Sorry. I have a couple of ranch calls to make this morning. Nothing strenuous or too far way, if you'd care to ride along with me," Matt said, cracking three eggs into the skillet, then dropping in some stick butter and a handful of vegetables he'd cut up earlier—cubanelle peppers, onions, mushrooms. "If you feel like you're up to it."

"A ride? Maybe that's a good way to start slowing down. I'm not used to doing things at a leisurely pace, so since you think I'll be OK…" Ellie shrugged. This wasn't what she'd had in mind but she was the intruder here. The choices weren't hers to make. Which was unusual, as in her real world all the choices *were* hers. Every last one of them. Yet right now, letting someone else step in was nice. It was almost like being on holiday. No worries. No concerns. No decisions.

Except… She placed her hand on her belly and felt a kick. The very first one. It caught her off guard because it hadn't happened before. But it was a good, sharp kick, and she gasped.

Immediately, Matt was at her side. "What?" he choked out, dropping to his knees, automatically taking hold of her wrist to take her pulse.

But she guided his hand to the spot where she'd felt the kick and smiled. "First kick," she whispered, amazed that she was suddenly on the verge of tears over something so ordinary. She was, though. Her lips were trembling when the second kick came, with Matt's hand pressed to her belly, then her tears started. Damned hormones.

"Strong one," he said, a look of amazement coming over his face. "And this was the first time?"

She nodded, sniffing back the tears. "She's been very quiet up until now."

"She?" he asked, refusing to move his hand from her belly. "You already know?"

"Not really. I've just assumed..."

Finally, he pulled away and stood. "With a kick like that, it's definitely a boy. Strong one. He's going to come out ready to play football." He backed away, saw that the scramble he'd been fixing had burned, and dumped it in the garbage.

"Women can be as strong as men," Ellie said, not quite ready to go take her shower now. Somehow, being connected here as a family of three seemed comforting. Cozy. It wouldn't last long, though. Everybody was caught up in a moment—and the moment would be over in a blink, and life would be back to where it had been. It was a complicated place to be in. But for now the fantasy of something she'd never had was settling over her, making her feel mellow. Would she ever have that? Or would her life be as it was now—all work, all the time?

"Sure they can. I've worked with some amazing women who were as strong as any man. But it still felt like the kick of a little boy to me."

Ellie laughed. "Wishful thinking, Doctor?"

"Not particularly," Matt said. Then suddenly that moment was over. His face darkened to almost a scowl and the look in his eyes went distant. "Look, I'd like to be out of here in thirty, if you're still interested in coming. My goal is to be back here by noon, grab Lucas, and see a couple of the locals this afternoon. After that, I do have one call later today, not out on a ranch. Shut-in who needs her medicine. You're welcome to come along on that, too, if you wish, since I promised Lucas we'd go to the Roadside for pizza afterwards." With that, he tossed the used dishtowel on the counter and headed toward the hall.

"Bring yourself some water. It can get hot out there. Oh, and two conditions. Let me examine you before we go. You showed up here exhausted and dehydrated and passed out yesterday, so I want to see if anything's off this morning. If it is, I'm going to suggest you go back to bed. Second, if you go, you sit. Nothing else. OK?"

"Are you saying pregnant woman aren't capable—?"

"No," he interrupted. "I know exactly what pregnant women are capable of doing. But since you haven't allowed me a good look at you, and I have an idea you're not going to, I just want to be careful. And it wasn't that long ago you passed out so, since that pregnancy is also mine, I don't want to take any chances. All I want to do, Ellie, is take care of you and the baby while you're here."

She did understand his concern because she was concerned as well. But being fussed over so much— she wasn't used to it. Her life was about taking charge, doing everything on her own. Then suddenly to turn part of herself over to someone else, even if only for a little while, was difficult. Went against her natural grain. But her life, right now, wasn't only about her, was it? It was also about the baby, which made it about Matt as well.

"I appreciate your concern," she said. "And I apologize if I seem...put off. I'm not. In fact, I'm grateful for what you're doing. I know my being here isn't easy for you, especially with the news I brought. So whatever you think you need to do..."

"How about we take this minute by minute?" he said. "I've got more going on than I ever thought I'd have, and for me it's mostly about improvising in the moment." Matt chuckled, finally lightening up. "Being in surgery wasn't as complicated as what I'm going through here. At least there I knew what to do. Here I haven't a clue, and it's a challenge I don't have a solution for yet."

"Well, get your stethoscope ready. I'll be back down here for my exam in fifteen minutes."

Ellie glanced back at Matt before she walked down the hall to the *casita*. He was heading toward the stairs, walking very rigidly. She'd never seen anyone so rigid before. But like he'd just told her, this situation was a challenge. She hadn't meant that to happen but, realistically, she should have expected it. Maybe she had, subconsciously. Because he was acting the way she would have, given the same circumstances—reluctantly. In her business world she didn't like reluctance, didn't deal with it too well.

But this wasn't her business world now, and she was beginning to see a side of life she'd never seen before. Matt was sacrificing a lot, staying here for Lucas. And here she was, asking him for an even greater sacrifice, then not being as cooperative as she should when he wasn't giving her what she wanted. She had to do better, and not just for the baby's sake. For Matt's as well. She genuinely cared for him. He was an honorable man, stuck in a very tough place. She'd seen that honor in Reno. But now, seeing him in this situation, she admired him. He was holding it together better than she would have.

Had she known him better when she'd made her decision to come here, she might not have come. But she was here and now, for the first time since she'd learned she was pregnant, this pregnancy wasn't just about her. She had to keep that in mind.

Matt looked in the dresser mirror and imagined a hundred tiny wrinkles had popped up around his eyes since yesterday. He wanted to kick something, or punch it so hard it smashed the bloody hell out of his knuckles— anything to make him feel something other than numb. But that's all he felt right now. Numb. Trying to be civil. Trying to hold it together—but not even sure *what* he was trying to hold together.

Six weeks ago, a soldier had been brought in on a stretcher, massive trauma below the waist. One leg gone above the knee, one leg hanging by a thread. No blood pressure to speak of. Massive bleed-out without the necessary replacement in store. Everything had been wrong with him. He shouldn't have lived. But he had.

They'd put in their time, not with much optimism, done everything humanly possible to save him, and while they'd sent him out with extensive damage, *they'd sent him out*. Miracle. He recalled celebrating that one with his colleagues. The ones who had been off duty had partied hard all night while he'd simply sat back, grateful another mother would have her son coming home. It was a feeling that always overwhelmed him.

Another soldier came through the door a few days later—had a little headache. They'd put him at the end of the list because he'd walked in on his own, was alert, joking, said all he needed were a couple of aspirin and he'd be good to get back out. Except ten minutes later he was lying dead in the entry hall. Healthy, to all outer appearances, and nothing wrong. But a bullet had ricocheted off his helmet, hadn't so much as touched his skin. Yet the impact had caused a brain bleed. No miracle there. And it hadn't made sense. Sometimes nothing did. And that had been the one he'd gotten drunk over. Had kicked a hole through the wall. Gone outside and screamed into the night for the uselessness of it all.

He felt like screaming now, being back in Forgeburn. Taking over a medical practice, even if only temporarily. Raising a child, again temporarily. Then finding out about his own child.

Matt wouldn't scream, of course. Or get himself drunk the way he had over the soldier with the headache. So that left feeling numb, and maybe that wasn't such a bad thing after all. He could just go through the motions, step by step, until something happened. Or until he knew what to do. But, damn—he wanted to kick something anyway. Which he did. The trash can sitting next to the dresser. Funny thing was, it had no effect on him. Nothing satisfying, nothing stress-busting. In fact, he felt foolish, which was just one step above feeling numb.

Now all he had to do was go for stupid, and he'd have the perfect triple. Why? Because she'd been here no longer than the blink of an eye and he was already having…feelings. Sure, in Reno he'd had feelings. But he chalked them up to what had been happening in the moment. They'd been good. No denying that. And he'd enjoyed her company. Sitting around talking and relaxing—it was something he never did. But with Ellie it had felt right.

Now, though... Matt took one last look in the mirror, not even sure he recognized the man looking back. "How could you even think about her that way?" he asked himself as he threw on a respectable, doctor-like shirt. "She was just someone to suit your mood. Someone convenient." Except, even as he said the words to his reflection, they stuck on his tongue, bitter and disgusting. Ellie wasn't like that. He'd known that from the start. So why was he trying so hard to convince himself otherwise now? "Because she scares you, McClain. Because she's *not* like the others."

That was true. She wasn't. But why did that make a difference? "Because you're stupid. Bingo! Triple."

The only problem was, caring for Ellie in any capacity didn't really make him feel stupid. It made him feel...alive. She was nice to look at. No denying the attraction. It had hit him hard and fast the first time he'd set eyes on her in Reno. And it hadn't been just her beauty that had attracted him. It had been her confidence. And the way she'd dealt with the people who'd stopped by her display. Everyone had been important to her. Everyone had received her beautiful smile. Even the ones he'd seen pestering her for something other than information about her services.

His keen attraction aside—and it was difficult putting it there—now that he was getting to know Ellie even better than he had after their two nights, he liked what he was discovering. Sure, she was stubborn. And used to having things her way. But that's what had made her successful. She was smart, too. The best part was, even though she might be resistant to his suggestions at first, she listened to reason. She wanted what was right for their baby and for that he loved her.

In the romantic, happily-ever-after sense? Admittedly, that had popped into his mind a time or two, even as far back as Reno. But common sense always took over. *It couldn't work.* As harsh as that seemed, it was true. Neither of them wanted *that* kind of relationship. No romance, they'd both said. Of course, they'd both said one night only, and look what had happened to that. Still, those two nights in Reno may have been the best nights of his life, but that's all they had been. Two nights in his life. Two nights like he'd never known before. Probably would never know again.

"OK, ready for your physical?" he asked Ellie, on his way down the stairs. She was dressed in a pair of loose-fitting khakis and a white cotton blouse meant to hide the baby bump. But now that he knew it was there, it was obvious to him.

"If you insist," she said, sounding surprisingly calm. "But I'm not undressing."

He chuckled. "Maybe that's something we should have considered a few weeks ago."

"As I recall, you weren't complaining," she said, holding out her arm as he wrapped an old-fashioned manual blood-pressure cuff around it.

"Soldier on leave first time in over a year. Surrounded by pretty women at a convention. What can I say?" He pumped up the cuff, listened, then deflated it. "What's your norm?" he asked.

"About one-ten over mid-seventies. Why?"

"Because, like yesterday, you're a little high. Still in the normal range, but high for your normal."

"Which really doesn't mean anything," Ellie defended.

"Says who?" he asked.

"I was an obstetrics nurse. I know these things."

Matt bent down and assessed her ankles and lower legs. "And I'm impressed by that how?"

"Do you work with obstetrics on the battlefield?"

"Sometimes."

"But it's not your specialty?"

"Never claimed it was. Where I work...let's just say I'm a jack-of-all-trades. I take whatever's thrown at me." From the very best of it to the very worst.

"Well, obstetrics *was* my specialty, and..."

He stood back up and took a penlight to examine her eyes. "And you're an illustrator now. Correct?"

"And videographer," she said, tilting her head back for his exam.

"Which doesn't exactly put you in the mainstream of current medicine," he said, clicking off his light then next examining her hands.

"Actually, it keeps me right in there since I'm the one who's doing the media that med students, residents and even fellows are studying. You, too, if you stay current with the journals. So I would say that makes me more current than most doctors."

He prodded her fingers for a moment then looked directly at her. "Guess that's a field I don't know much about. You'll have to tell me more when we have time. Now, give me your physician's contact number. I want to talk to him before I turn you loose to do something crazy."

Ellie looked instantly alarmed and her face drained of nearly all color. "What's wrong?" she sputtered.

"Nothing that I can see," Matt said, instantly regretting his lack of bedside manner. "Look, I'm sorry for being so—abrupt. I've never had a bedside manner, never had to. My patients come and go faster than you can imagine, and I rarely get to speak to them. My work is concentrated solely on getting the problem in front of me fixed. So I know sometimes I come on too strong and—"

"Strong? *You come on too strong?*" She held out her wrist. "Take my pulse and feel what your coming on too strong has done to me. That kind of bedside manner out here isn't going to work, Matt. I don't know battlefield medicine. Can't even begin to imagine what it's like out there for you, and I'm not going to judge you for your abruptness. But you're not out there right now. And I don't mean to be critical, but you really do need to concentrate on being...personable."

He chuckled. "Personable?"

"Friendly. Smile. You know, the way you were in Reno."

"Ah, yes. Me in seduction mode."

"Which worked," she said.

"Apparently. Anyway, do you always try to fix things like the way you're trying to fix my bedside manner?" he asked.

"Yes. It's what I do. Most people would call it second nature or something like that, but for me it's my first nature. I have a lot of people working for me around the world and I have to make sure everything stays fixed all the time." She smiled sheepishly. "I guess I was the one coming on too strong, wasn't I?"

"Look. We're in an awkward spot here. You know it, and I know it. We're both nervous. I'm not sure either one of knows what to do, or even how to go about starting to figure it out. It's going to take some time to get it all sorted, so how about we just make the best of it for now? Maybe be friends?"

"Sure, friends," she said.

Seeing the sudden look of sadness come over her, Matt walked over to her and wrapped his arms around her. "We'll get you through this, Ellie. Not sure how but, I promise, you're not alone."

"I'm always alone, Matt. And I didn't come here because I wanted someone to take care of me." She sniffled. "I really wanted to do the right thing."

"I appreciate it. Not sure what to do with it but, for what it's worth, I really do appreciate it."

Ellie sniffled once more, then pulled away from him. "You've got appointments, and I'd like to go, so if you need to call my doctor in Reno…" She brought up Doc Shaffer's number on her phone and handed it to him. He took it then wandered down the hall for some privacy. Three minutes later he returned. "Gestational diabetes?" he asked.

"Not diagnosed, no symptoms. My mother had it, and she's a Type-One diabetic, so naturally he's worried about me. Which is why I'm spot on nutritionally with everything I need to be. It's not a condition, Matt, until it is. So far, I'm good." She brushed the last of her tears off her cheeks.

"But you didn't tell me."

"Tell you what? A list of everything I don't have?"

"He said you were as stubborn as they came."

"But did he say I'm healthy enough to go out on this ride with you?"

"He said, and I quote, 'She'll do what she wants to

do. I told her to go home and rest for a day but, apparently, she took a ten-hour drive and passed out in your exam because she wouldn't even stop long enough to buy a drink. That's who she is.' Which tells me that you're a royal pain." He said it with a smile on his face because under different circumstances he was sure he'd like the challenge of her. Right now, though, it worried him.

"I'm determined, Matt. There's a difference. What I do has a purpose. Being a royal pain is simply for fun and pleasure."

He chuckled. "So, this is how it's going to be?"

She smiled back at him. "How about I work on *my* bedside manner, too. Although you didn't complain about it in Reno, did you?"

His response was to groan. "Like I said, you're along for the ride *only*. Nothing else." Words easier said than done. He knew that. Knew that, with Ellie, he had a whole new level of headache to add to the ones already stacking up on him.

The first few miles took them down the highway. Smooth road. Beautiful scenery, with all the cacti in bloom. Ellie had read that this was such a good bloom year that all the vibrant colors were visible by satellite. She didn't doubt it. While Reno was on the edge of the desert, this was different. More remote. More raw. Wild. Stunning in a way she'd never expected, given that she'd never been here before. "It's amazing," she said, finally settling in, still feeling the tingle of Matt's touch as he'd examined her. She rubbed her arms briskly as the goose-bumps reappeared simply from the memory. "Prettier than any garden I've ever seen."

"You chilly?" he asked.

"Nope," she lied. "Just enjoying the scenery."

"Well, the spring colors were one of the few things I liked when I lived here. That, and all the rocks and canyons where you could climb."

"You liked to climb?"

"Still do. Just haven't had the opportunity for, well—since I moved away. Did have some training in the army, which wasn't much of a deal considering all the real climbing I was used to."

"Maybe when you're here, you'll be able to get some in." She looked off in the distance at the red rock that seemed to be jutting out of nowhere. What would it be like to be able to simply go up the side of it? In her life, there had never been time for activities or athletics or anything like that. She'd had meal time, and tutoring time, play time, reading time, bedtime. On the weekends, but not too often, she'd been granted mother time, maybe an hour or two when she'd been allowed to tag along with her mother on appointments. But never time to simply go climb a rock or look at pretty flowers.

So maybe Matt didn't have the best of it here—she really didn't know that story, or maybe he'd been so overwhelmed he hadn't known how to look for the best of what he'd had. Whatever the case, she was enjoying the ride, enjoying the image in her mind of him climbing up one of those gigantic rocks.

"I hope so. Although I'll be out of shape."

"You look in pretty good shape to me," she blurted out, even though she hadn't meant to.

"Army life will do that to you. But if I keep up my cowboy medicine for long…" Matt sighed heavily. "They'll probably have to put me back through some

basic training before they let me back out on the battlefield again."

"You really do want to go back to the battlefield?
I've consulted with several military medical person-
nel who couldn't wait until their rotation was over. All
of them said the work got to them, so many casualties
and things that couldn't get fixed. And the gunfire in
the distance. Or never knowing when the hospital might
come under siege or they might have to evacuate. It was
a consistent story, Matt. And here you are, totally the
opposite. So why?"

"Because somebody has to do it, and I can. I do well
under pressure. And I can shut out pretty much everything but what I'm doing at the moment. I got used to
doing that when I was a kid. My old man yelled a lot. I
learned to shut him out and concentrate on something
else. Guess it carried over with me to the military."
He slowed the truck, then made a right-hand turn onto
something that once might have been called a road.
Today it was barely a path with some gravel. Winding
for miles. No end in sight. The sign at the turn-off read
only "Tolly Ranch Road."

"Tolly?" she asked. "They give these roads names?"

"Nope. Tolly is my patient. His trailer is at the end
of the road. Only one out this way. So the names you
see on the roads are actually the names of the people
who live on them. Normally, it's one person or family
per road."

"And these roads are how long?"

"Sometimes eight, maybe ten miles."

"With no one else living on it."

"No one, and nothing. It's deserted out here, Ellie.
Lonely. Barren."

"Why do they stay?"

"Open grazing for their cattle. They don't have to own the land. They can lease it from the government, and the cost is a fraction of what they'd have to pay to buy it and pay the taxes. The stipulation is they must have a base from which to operate, and since they don't own the property they won't build on it because, technically, what they might build there would belong to the government as it's on government-owned property. Hence the cowboy trailers. They're not permanent. Rundown, yes, since they're not permanent residences and usually just a place to sleep for the night. But they serve their purpose."

As they proceeded down Tolly Ranch Road, Matt slowed the truck to almost a crawl. It was only precautionary, as the road wasn't bumpy like many of them were. "This is a pretty good road—Doc Granger left a road evaluation with each patient chart, so I'd know what I might be getting myself into. Some will be truckworthy, others I can take a motorcycle, and some may require a horse. This is one of the better ranch roads, but just in case, there's a pillow in the back you can use if you need to support your back. And if it gets too rough, tell me."

"Thanks," she said, grabbing hold of the pillow because, yes, she was starting to have back spasms. She'd had them before—nothing serious. And these, right now, weren't too bad. But just in case... "As long as what I do doesn't put the baby at risk, everything's fine."

"*Our* baby," he reminded her.

That it was. *Their* baby. And the sound of it wasn't so bad. In fact, she rather liked it. Of course, that wasn't going to happen, not in the real sense. Still—she shut her eyes and for a moment envisioned a pink, frilly nursery. Pretty little-girl clothes hanging in the closet. Stuffed animals and dolls everywhere. And a music box with a ballerina spinning and spinning and spinning inside, like the one her nanny had given her, and her mother had taken away because it had been too foolish for *her* child.

For a moment, a melancholy mood slipped down over Ellie and she was sitting in a rocking chair in that nursery, holding her baby. But her mother's words came back to haunt her—*too foolish*. And the image disappeared. But was it foolish? Nothing inside her told her it wasn't, but nothing inside her told her it was either. She liked the dream, though. It made her feel contented in a way nothing else did.

"So, how far off the road is Tolly?" she asked, opening her eyes and trying to concentrate on the scenery.

"We go just a couple miles on this road, then we take a cut-off back about another five. Are you *sure* you're OK?" he asked, slowing the truck even more as a black-and-white cow wandered to the side of the road and simply stood there, looking at them. Ellie grabbed her phone and took a picture before they proceeded. "Maybe this wasn't such a good idea, bringing you with me," he continued.

"Like I said, I'm fine. Glad to get out and see all this. I never have time to just…look."

He smiled. "You know, if you weren't pregnant, we'd be out on my motorcycle."

"Might be fun, if you don't mind the weather. Me, I like my air-conditioning and creature comforts. Nice sound system, contoured seats, a little extra lumbar support. But that's not you, is it? You get along differently."

"See those abandoned house trailers over there?" he asked, slowing even more as they passed a small community of about thirty or forty abandoned structures sitting off by themselves. They were all falling down, rusted, looked as if they hadn't seen true care or maintenance for a couple decades.

"Yes. Why?"

"That's sort of a dumping ground for cowboy trailers that have gotten too rundown. They drag them down here and leave them. It's a small patch of private land and they pay the owner a dumping fee. He scraps what he can, sells parts, does some recycling. It's also where I come from. Lived there from the time I was ten or eleven until I left home when I was sixteen—one trailer or another. Lived in a storage shed a couple miles from here for a year before that, and in the back of my dad's car even before that. That's the difference between your world and mine, Ellie. Yours had air-conditioning and creature comforts. Mine didn't even have running water. In fact, we were merely squatters moving from trailer to trailer, always hoping for one that didn't have a leaking roof or holes in the floor."

"From what you'd said, I knew it was bad, but I didn't know how bad," Ellie said, taking one look at the trailer dump, then turning her head. She couldn't picture Matt there. Or anyone. "How did you get by?" she asked.

"Any way we could. Didn't always have food, but there were people who'd see me or Janice on the street and invite us in for a meal. Plus, we got handouts at the diner. And when we were in school, there was always a hot meal."

"But the other things—clothes, bathing."

"We took what we could, wherever we could get it.

People gave us hand-me-downs. We could bathe in the sink at the gas station." Matt's face betrayed no emotion. Not a flinch, not a frown. "It's what we knew."

"But didn't you also know how other people lived?" she asked, looking for a sign of some feeling yet not seeing it there.

"We did. But we also knew who we were—the two kids who lived at the dump. I got along, but Janice…"

There it was, a quick softening in his eyes. Then a flash of pain. Now, more than ever, she understood why Matt was being so particular about Lucas. He didn't want him to end up here, the way his mother had. "Did she ever get out?" Ellie asked.

"For a while. We didn't keep in touch, so I don't know the details other than she started here then ended here."

That flash of pain again. Ellie's heart broke for him. He carried the guilt of his sister, probably had done ever since he'd been a boy. She laid a hand on Matt's forearm and gave him a squeeze "I'm sorry about…"

He laid *his* hand atop hers for a moment, then pulled it back, and sped up once they were past the little settlement. She was too stunned by his honesty to know how to respond, so she simply looked at the road ahead, thinking about their differences and similarities. He'd come from nothing while she'd had everything. Yet they both grown up so—alone. No one to care, no one to comfort them. And here they were now, with a child on the way, wondering what was best for him or her. Better than either of them had had—that's what would be best.

But wasn't that really just giving up their child to someone they could only hope would provide better? Her ideas about adoption were changing because being around Matt made this whole situation feel more real. Before, it had been an intellectual issue—her safe place. Always deferring to what she knew best.

Except that's not what she was doing here. Something was turning around in Ellie. Her convictions were weakening. The intellectual was giving way to the emotional, try as hard as she could to stop it. But she couldn't, and she wasn't going to blame it on being hormonal. She also wasn't going to admit that to Matt, because she wasn't ready to acknowledge these new thoughts to herself yet. "How did that happen?" she finally asked. "How did you end up living like that?"

"No mother. An old man who didn't work but loved what he found in the bottom of a booze bottle. No one who cared whether two little kids were fed, or clean, or went to school." Once they were out of sight of the run-down clump of trailers, he turned onto the next road they came to.

"And the owner didn't say anything?"

"The owner was required to have someone on the property. He sure as hell didn't want to be there, so he used my dad's name in exchange for letting my dad have free access to whatever piece of rubbish trailer he wanted to stay in for a while. And I'm not telling you this because I expect pity, or any other kind of emotion from you. It's so you'll understand why I'm not giving you what I'm assuming you'd hoped would be a fast decision about the baby. I don't make fast decisions. Had too many of those made for me over my life, and they didn't always turn out well. In fact, *most* of them didn't when I was younger."

This wasn't the way she'd wanted this conversation to go. Wasn't at all how she'd expected it to happen. "You know, Matt, when I came here I thought since you were in a medical practice, that you'd left the military, or I wouldn't have even…"

The truth be told, she'd never really given herself over to the possibility that Matt might not want things to work out the way she did. Of course, that was the way she lived her life, ran her business, always got ahead. Ellie assumed herself into what she wanted, then worked hard to get it. Just like she'd assumed Matt would want to raise his child. Except she was pretty sure he didn't, and there was nothing inside her that wanted to work hard to make it happen.

For whatever reason, Matt was bringing out a softer side to her she'd never seen before. And that new side clearly didn't want her to do what she normally did. "I don't want to tear up your life," she said simply.

"I never thought you did," he said. "I had a right to know, and be involved. I'm glad you didn't take that away from me. Not sure what to do with that right, though, because if you do go through with your own plans not to raise our child, it puts me in a tough spot."

It's your way, Ellie. Only your way. You don't need anybody else. Grow up and be a strong woman on your own. You don't need a man to prove anything to or about.

Her mother's words, her mother's sentiments. But her mother was so wrong. In fact, Ellie felt anything but that strong woman she'd been raised to believe in. And all because she was seeing something she hadn't expected to see—a man she simply hadn't expected. One who'd literally risen from the ashes. A man she was glad was the father of her baby. "Look, I don't want to pressure you into anything, Matt. That was never my intention. I'm a straightforward businesswoman in everything I do, and I couldn't have done otherwise with our situation."

"I appreciate your honesty, but you have to know the honest side of me. I'm going back into the military. Back to being a battlefield surgeon, as I've mentioned. And I can't do that and be a single father. The only reason I'm here now is to make sure Lucas ends up in the best situation possible. I owe that to my sister. The plan was that we'd always get out of here together. The agreement was that the first one to get away would save up until there was enough money to bring the other one along. I was the first one out. Had a few dollars—not enough to get us both out but enough to get me to Vegas. Unfortunately, it took me longer than I thought it would, and by the time I was in a position to help her, I was in the military, finally doing something with my life. And she'd given up waiting. I lost track of her, then got sidetracked with my military duty as well as going to school…"

Matt paused, took a deep breath and let it out slowly. "Bottom line, I got my life, she got cancer and died. So, that's where I am right now. Doing for my sister what I should have done a long time ago, and didn't. Which may make me look like the perfect person to raise our baby. But I'm not. I'm only fulfilling a promise I didn't keep by making sure Lucas gets what Janice never had—a good life. I'm sure that isn't what you want to hear, but I can't be any less honest with you than you were with me. I know you came here looking for a full-time daddy, but it's not me, Ellie. I'm sorry."

Now she was discouraged. Even on the verge of tears. Hormones again? Maybe, maybe not. But just for a little while she'd hoped—well, it didn't matter what she'd hoped, did it? A home and family. That proverbial house with the white picket fence. She'd seen that for a moment with Matt in Reno, and while that life was never her plan, every now and then she'd caught herself wrapped up in that daydream. With Matt, because he wasn't the kind of man she typically dealt with. They all had agendas, while all she could see in Matt was honor. More now than before. But she was wrong about that plan of hers, where he would raise their child and someday, in some small way, maybe even include her in their child's life.

Disappointed in a way she hadn't expected to be, Ellie slid down in the truck seat, readjusted the pillow, punched it, folded it, punched it some more, and when she couldn't find a way to make it comfortable, she opened the truck window, threw it out, and spent the last minutes of the truck ride fighting back the hormonal overflow she would not let him see. Not one burning drop of it.

CHAPTER FOUR

ELLIE WAS FIGHTING SOMETHING, and it frustrated Matt to know he was the cause of it. He hadn't meant to do that, hadn't meant to just blurt out everything. But he had, and there was no going back now. She wasn't going to get what she'd come here for and, for some reason, even though he'd caused her mood, what he wanted to do was pull off the road and simply hold her in his arms. Protect her. Comfort her.

It wasn't a reaction he'd normally have after being so blunt, but Ellie was different, and she caused different feelings and emotions in him. Because of the baby? Maybe. But also because of her. She seemed like she was always at odds with something in her life, and that was a very tough life to lead. He'd lived it himself for a long time. But he'd found his way. Had Ellie, though? She claimed she had with this business she owned, but he wasn't so sure because she seemed so exposed to things that hurt or discouraged her. And fought so hard against them.

He'd seen some of that in Reno—she had tried to be so serious even when they'd been in bed. Fighting hard not to show pleasure, even though it had shown through when she'd let down her guard. He smiled, thinking about that first night and her bravado—*I'm ready when you are,* she'd said as she'd stood across the room from him, practically hiding behind the armoire. He'd wanted to see her step away from that armoire but with respect to her shyness he'd turned off the lights and waited until she'd slipped under the sheets next to him. She hadn't been tentative then, as he'd expected her to be. In fact, she had been wild, like no other woman in his life had ever been.

The second night had caught him off guard. Ellie had been in his room in bed, waiting, when Matt had come back from the convention. No guards up this time. But they'd talked first. Mostly about insignificant things— at least, insignificant as far as they were concerned. Which had been when he'd discovered he really liked Ellie. In fact, if his situation in the army hadn't been so difficult, he might have asked to see her again. But he hadn't because he was going straight back to the war, and he didn't need the distraction of worrying about the woman he'd left behind, or if she'd be there waiting for him when he finally returned stateside.

But that second morning Ellie had seemed different. Not subdued so much as thoughtful. Maybe even a little sad as she'd stood at the window, looking out, all wrapped up in the bed sheet, and had said, *It's too bad this can't be real life.* He'd caught a glimpse of a vulnerability, much like the one he'd caught their first night together when she'd hidden herself behind the armoire, and both nights he'd wondered how someone so successful and forthright in the business world could almost shrink away when she stepped out of it.

Now he saw that vulnerability again, and she didn't

even seem to be trying to hide it. "Is there anything I can do? Anything at all?" he finally asked in desperation.

"I'm fine," she said, her voice on the verge of sounding sad.

"You don't look fine, and you're not acting fine." He stopped the truck, reached over the seat and grabbed hold of his jacket. "You can use this as a pillow until we…find the one you tossed out on our way back or buy another one."

"I don't need a pillow, Matt."

"Look, Ellie, I know what this is about, and I'm sorry. But I'm not the one, and it's better you know now because that will give you more time to figure out what to do." Damn, he hated this. Hated every bit of it. But his life wouldn't accommodate what she wanted.

"Us, Matt. More time for *us* to figure out what to do."

"Did you really expect to show up on my doorstep, tell me you've got a baby for me to raise, then walk away from it?"

"I don't know what I expected," she admitted. "But I guess that's close enough."

"Well, you're right about one thing. It *is* something we need to figure out together." He was beginning to feel as discouraged as she sounded because this baby was his responsibility as well as Ellie's. And that's the one thing he had to keep in mind—it was Ellie's responsibility, too.

Even so, as sad as she looked, he really did want to put his arms around her and tell her things would be OK. Somehow, though, he didn't think that would be an appreciated gesture. "This first stop, like I said, is Tolly. John Tolly. Chronic backache, according to his chart. He stays in his trailer a good bit of the time, and usually

gets seen whenever the doctor—which would be me—
can catch up with him. According to the chart, it's been
going on for a couple of years, intermittently. He's not
agreeable to therapy or medication. Any ideas?" Sure,
he was grasping now, but anything to connect to her
was good, because she seemed so far away.

"He could be sitting badly in his saddle," Ellie finally commented. "It happens. They get old. The leather
wears one way or another, throws the body out of alignment."

Stopping the truck in front of Tolly's trailer, Matt
grabbed his medical bag and hopped out. "How would
you know that?"

"Did a video about a year ago that featured uncom-
mon ailments in a variety of workers who spend their
lives outside, doing hard labor. Crooked saddle was one
of them. It gets you in the lower back mostly."

"And the cure?" he asked, totally impressed.

"Either have the old saddle straightened—there are
people who specialize in that—or get a new one." She
rose up, looked at the old trailer sitting just in front of
her, then slid back down in the seat. "Tell John Tolly
a crooked saddle can be bad for his horse, too. Same
thing—it gets them in the muscles." With that, she laid
her head against the back of the truck seat and closed
her eyes.

It wasn't much, Matt thought as he crossed the dirt
expanse from the truck to the trailer, where John Tolly
was standing outside, waiting for him, but it was a start.
It had drawn her out of her slump for a moment or two.
And she'd just made what could be a major diagnosis seem like she was simply telling a children's story.
Once upon a time there was back ache. "Check the

saddle," said the nurse. And the doctor did. The nurse
was right. The saddle was crooked. Then the cowboy
was cured, and everybody was happy.

Everybody but the nurse, and for that he did feel bad.

"So, how long have you had backache this time?"
Matt asked the old cowboy, after an exam of the usual—
vital signs, joints, reflexes—but everything normal for a
man who'd lived a hard, sixty-three-year life. "Because,
according to my charts, it's been going on for a couple
of years, with no relief."

"Old age, Doc. It's creeping up on me. What can I
say? It happens to the best of them, and I sure as hell
don't come close to the best of them." He pulled up his
shirt for Matt to have a look at his back, and winced
when Matt applied a hard thumb to John's extensor
muscles.

"Trouble getting up from a standing position?" Matt
asked, continuing his exam.

"Sometimes. But I manage."

"And lifting?"

"Can't lift as much as I used to but, at my age who
can?" He winced again when Matt singled out his
obliques and applied pressure.

"And you've been taking…" Matt grabbed his tablet and tapped the cursor, sending up the part of John's
chart for medications. "Nothing at all"

"Don't like pills. Won't take them," John said, sitting
up on his bed and buttoning his shirt. "Told that to the
old doc, telling you the same thing. No pills. No shots."

"And I don't suppose you'd finally consent to physical therapy? Maybe some tests at the hospital?"

"Had some tests. They were negative. And the near-
est place to get therapy is a hundred miles from here.

How many times a week would you suggest I drive that, Doc? How many times a week would you suggest I neglect my cattle to go get my back rubbed?" He pushed himself off the bed, ever so slowly, then headed to the front of the trailer. It was a one-room deal. Bed at the back, small kitchen area at the front, a seating area near the center where there was barely enough room to sit.

Very compact and, to Matt, very claustrophobic and filled with bad memories. "How often are you out on the range?" he asked, typing some notes into his tablet trying to ignore the resemblance of this trailer to the ones he'd lived in. It was difficult, though. Everything surrounding him brought back bad memories...memories he'd have to put aside to do this job.

"Out for three, then here for two. But when I stay here, that's not to rest. It's to get myself ready to go out again. Try to get myself back to my real house a couple days a month, when I can."

What a hard life, Matt thought as he slipped his tablet into his medical bag, then pulled out some vials as well as a sample container. "Mind if I do a few tests?"

"Help yourself, but what you're looking for isn't there. The other doc took samples every time he was out here and all he could prove was that, except for a bad back, I'm healthier than a sixty-three-year-old man has a right to be."

"Still got a job to do, John," Matt said, as he took blood samples, then labeled them when John went to render up that other sample. Several minutes later the men walked outside together, but Matt stopped short of the truck, glad to get out of the trailer before he started breaking out in a cold sweat, and noticed the horse tied to the fence not too far from the trailer. "You still go out on a horse?" he asked. Some still did. Many did not. All-terrain vehicles were taking over the aspect of being a cowboy as often as not.

"Every chance I get. Some of the ground isn't fit, but a good bit of it is, so I do it the old-fashioned way."

"Would you mind saddling up for me?"

"Any reason why?" John asked, frowning.

"Something someone told me about crooked saddles. They can cause backache. Ever heard of it?"

John shook his head. And as he did so, Ellie stepped into view. "It's not common," she said, "but it happens often enough that there are saddle specialists out there who can fix most saddles, if they're not too badly out of alignment."

"Well, the one I've got is older than dirt," he said, extending his hand to Ellie. "John Tolly, ma'am."

"Ellie Landers," she said.

Matt noted that her face was pleasant now, the scowl gone. The rigid body had disappeared. This was the Ellie he'd met that night. The one he'd taken to immediately. "Ellie's a friend, and a very good nurse, out for the ride with me today."

"Can I offer you something to drink, Ellie? I have some fresh tea, cold water—or I can make you some lemonade."

She held up her water bottle. "I'm good. But thanks."

"Well, then, guess, I'll mount up and see if I've got that crooked saddle thing going on." With that, John wandered over to a shed that was better built than his trailer to get his saddle.

"You feeling better?" Matt asked.

"I get these—I suppose you could call them hormonal surges. They make me emotional, and not in a good way. Sorry about your pillow, by the way."

Matt chuckled. "I'm just glad it wasn't anything important."

"So, do you think it's his saddle?" she asked.

"Your guess is as good as mine. He's been seen for his back for quite a while, and nothing turns up. I'm hoping it's something as simple as he's sitting skew. Any other guesses? Or videos that might give a clue?"

Ellie rubbed her hand along her own lower back. "Nope. Just sympathy pains."

"Your back hurt?" he asked, suddenly concerned.

"Not really. Just a little twinge now and then. Nothing to be concerned about. My doctor said a lot of pregnant women suffer back pain, and I suppose I'm one of those."

But she wasn't showing that much yet, and the additional weight of the baby wasn't pulling on her spine. So, unless she was subject to back pain as a rule, this seemed off. "And you didn't tell me?" He wasn't sure what to do now. Take Ellie back to the house where she could rest, or continue to his next appointment? If he took her back, it would put him off his schedule for the rest of the day, and he wouldn't have time for Lucas later this evening. But if Ellie was having problems...

"Like I said, many pregnant women get aches and pains, Matt. I'm fine. And, trust me, I'm not going to do anything to put this baby at risk. You have my word on that."

"You didn't have back pain before you were pregnant?"

"No. In fact, I ran every morning and worked out

four times a week to keep myself in shape. Like my doc back home told me, it's just part of the process."

A part that had him worried. "Are you sure you're OK, because I could—?"

Ellie laid a reassuring hand on his arm. "I'm fine. Promise."

Matt still wasn't convinced. Of course, he didn't know if that was coming from a doctor's point of view or a nervous father's. A father's point of view—in a way, he liked that. So far, this baby wasn't all that real for him. He knew it existed, that Ellie carried it. But the idea of being a father to—him or her—hadn't sunk in, other than knowing it wouldn't work out in his life. Lucas deserved better. His child deserved better. *His child...*

A check of John Tolly on his saddle was all it took for Matt to conclude that his saddle was the cause of his pain. "You're sitting way off to the left," he said, checking the view from both sides then the rear. "Which means that until you get it fixed, or have a new one made, take your truck. And it probably wouldn't hurt to get a lumbar support cushion for that."

"You saying my bones are getting too old to work?" John asked, as he climbed down off the saddle.

"I'm saying your equipment is too old. Get it fixed or replace it, give it a month then call me for another appointment." If he'd even be here in another month. He'd heard a couple of his buddies were going back over to Afghanistan—he wanted to ship out with them. There was an opening and it was his, if he got his home situation straightened out. But that was the big question, wasn't it? Could he get his home situation straightened out? Especially in only a month?

Sighing, Matt helped Ellie situate herself back in the truck, then he climbed into the driver's seat. "Maybe you should be the one running the medical practice out here instead of me."

"Hard to do when the people would expect more than a camera or a sketch pad."

"So, what made you change—well, not careers so much, since what you do is medical? But direction. I know your company's successful. I looked it up on the internet. Didn't you like nursing?"

Ellie settled into the seat as they set off down the dusty road. "Actually, I loved being a nurse. But it wasn't the kind of responsibility I wanted to take on. Probably because I didn't believe I was good enough. Whatever the case, that's the way my life has always been—finding one thing but looking for something else, someplace where I fit in better. So I was looking around at various options, given the education I already had, and medical illustration caught my attention. I'm an artist—at least as a hobby. Put that together with my medical background, and it just seemed to suit me. I'd still be in the medical field but I'd be doing something that took into consideration other passions I had."

"So you simply started a company?" He'd read that, seen the high praise for how she'd built the company from the ground up and become a major competitor in her field in only a few short years. Even though it had nothing to do with him, it did make him proud of her.

"After another couple of years of education and a lot of extra study on running a business. It's a relatively small field but very demanding. Four-year undergrad degree in a science discipline, two more years on top of that in applied medical illustration. Some business education thrown in. I was late when I finally got to the table, but I worked hard and fast to get us up and going, and I landed my first significant contract within the first six months, and my first major contract inside my first year. All that allowed me to grow my business, which is what I've been trying to do every day since I started it."

Ellie shifted positions again, favoring her back. He noticed it, and it worried him. "So, you're a career woman, one hundred percent."

"Competing in a corporate world that's largely owned by men. It's a hard battle sometimes." She smiled, and her nose wrinkled. "But I usually win."

"From what I read, your services are in pretty high demand." Matt liked the confidence he was hearing in her voice. This was a side of Ellie he hadn't seen, and it fit her well. The way her blue eyes lit up when she talked about her work, the enthusiasm that emanated from her—it was sexy in a way he'd never thought sexy could be. Her sexiness was more than simply her physical attributes—which were very nice. It was a package deal. Intellect, ambition, competitive edge. She had it all, and another time, another place...

The second ranch call went quickly, and before Ellie knew it, they were on their way back to Matt's house. It was about a thirty-mile drive, which wasn't all that long unless your back was spasming off and on, like hers was. "Matt, what do you know about relaxin?" she asked, as he slowed to avoid a pothole.

"Not a lot other than it's a hormone that lets the ligaments in the pelvic area relax, and the joints to loosen up in preparation for the birth process. The problem is, relaxin can also cause those ligaments to loosen too much, which causes back pain. Sometimes muscle separation. Is that what you think your back pain is coming from?"

"Maybe. I looked it up on the internet and it just made me wonder if I have some kind of imbalance."

"Well, relaxin isn't usually considered a complication unless there's an abundance of it. Has your OB/GYN checked that?"

"He's done routine blood counts but that's all."

"Well, how about I order in what I need for the test and we'll see if that's what's causing your pain? Because if it is…"

Ellie knew the rest of what Matt was going to say. An over-abundance of relaxin put her at risk for a miscarriage or an early delivery since her body was in the delivery mode due to the relaxin. "If it is, I could be in trouble."

"Which is why it's better to check it now, before we do anything else."

"Thank you," she said.

"What for?"

"For saying we. It makes me feel less alone in this. And less worried."

"You're not alone, Ellie. I may not be good for much else, but I'm not going to let you do this all by yourself." Which meant—well, he'd cross that army bridge when he came to it. Right now, his only concern was Ellie.

CHAPTER FIVE

ELLIE DROPPED DOWN onto her temporary bed in Matt's *casita*, not so much physically worn out as emotionally battered from the back-and-forth she was playing with herself. She'd been quite set in what she'd wanted when she'd arrived here, and every hour since seemed to have eroded bits and pieces of her resolve.

She was discovering how much she cared for this isolated man. He was the handsome, daring prince of every little girl's dreams, and he was the steady, noble man of most women's grown-up dreams. Certainly, he was the dream she'd fought against for a lifetime. And, no, that wasn't a hormonal surge leading her in that direction.

She'd watched him re-stitch a cowboy's dirty old wound this afternoon, taking care to get it clean and stitch it as neatly as he could, considering how the cowboy had first stitched it himself with regular thread and a sewing needle. It had been infected. Matt had given him antibiotics. It might require another open-up and a second good cleansing. Matt had made an appointment to meet him in ten days. The cowboy had initially been grumpy and resistant, only giving in to a doctor's exam at the insistence of his wife. But when they'd left, he had been laughing with Matt, recalling his own army days and inviting him back for a meal any time he was in the area.

Then Ellie had spent two hours in clinic with him, watching a handful of people come and go. All locals with simple complaints, all made to feel special by Matt's way. He wasn't overly friendly. He definitely kept a professional distance, was quite obviously trying hard to improve his bedside manner, and he was succeeding in making them feel the way she was feeling now. That was a gift she thought Matt was only now discovering in himself. Maybe it was the gift that had initially attracted her to him that night in Reno because for her to have done what she had with a stranger—that wasn't her. Not at all.

Whatever the case, Ellie was glad to be back here. Glad to hear Matt and Lucas playing in the other part of the house. The little boy still hadn't talked, but the way he automatically clung to Matt's hand and tried to walk the way Matt did, in long, deliberate strides, touched her heart. Everything about the special uncle-nephew relationship touched her heart, which made her long for the same for their child. And, perhaps, for her?

Of course, she was emotionally sloppy right now. Another time, another situation and none of this would have phased her. At least, she didn't think it would. She was a businesswoman who belonged in the business world. That's where she fit. Where she was comfortable. Although she wasn't quite as connected to that life as she had been yesterday. That would change, though. After she left here. After she got back to normal.

"Well, we have some dinner choices," Matt said, poking his head through Ellie's open *casita* door.

"Anything's fine with me," she said, lifting her head

off the pillow only to see Matt *and* Lucas standing in her doorway, same exact pose, with Lucas imitating Matt. "I'll even eat a little meat protein, if you think I need to."

"I'm not going to compromise your eating sensibilities unless I have to. Right now, I don't have to. But it's not about the food. I've thrown some various things together for a picnic. So, what's up here is where, exactly, we're going to have that picnic. My suggestion is the patio. Lucas wants to go up to the flat. You get to decide between the two."

Ellie sat up in bed. "First, what's the flat?"

"It's an area up the path from the house, a short hike away. If you're rested enough, it should be easy. And the view is amazing—it looks out over the valley. It's beautiful at sunset. Lucas likes to go up there, take along some toys and play in the rocks."

"And he told you that's where he wants to go?"

"Not in words. But in the way Lucas tells me other things he wants me to know."

"Which is how?"

"Mostly by being observant. I asked him where he'd like to picnic, and he looked up at the flats. It's in his eyes a lot of the time. You just have to understand what his eyes are saying."

Eyes so much like Matt's that Lucas could easily be mistaken for his son. Would *their* child have those same beautiful eyes? Ellie hoped so. "Well, if you think I'm good to go, and that's where Lucas wants to go…" She scooted to the side of the bed, ready to stand.

"It's up to you, Ellie. Only you know how you're feeling."

Down in the dumps, emotionally. That was how she

was feeling. "I'd like to see the sunset." And she wanted to spend time with Matt and Lucas, pretend they were a family. If only for a little while.

"Seriously, this is the walk a lot of doctors would prescribe for mild exercise. And if you have any trouble, you've got two big, strong men there to help you. Isn't that right, Lucas?" Matt asked, tousling the boy's hair.

Lucas looked up at Ellie for a moment, then switched his attention back to Matt. The little boy adored him so much. It was obvious to her, and it had to be obvious to Matt as well. Matt's decision to have him adopted— was that breaking his heart, because she knew it would break Lucas's heart once they were separated. And *their* baby—would she or he, in some unexplainable way, experience the pain of separation the way Lucas would? The way *she* would?

Suddenly, Ellie didn't feel so good, and all she wanted to do was go back to bed, pull the covers up over her head and blot out everything. Pretend she wasn't here. Pretend she wasn't carrying Matt's child. Pretend her life was the same as it used to be. Pretend. A nice place to go, but you couldn't stay there. Not when you were falling in love with your baby, and maybe also falling in love with your baby's father. There was nothing pretend about that.

"What I need is two big, strong men to lead the way, since I don't know where I'm going," she said, sitting up then tying on her hiking boots—boots that Matt had stopped and bought her earlier. Had he done that because he'd planned walks with her, not just this once but afterwards? He'd bought her a nice hiking jacket, too, with big pockets. The thought that he might want her to stay gave her an unexpected jolt. Would she stay if he asked her?

"I think we can manage that," Matt said, scooping Lucas up into his arms then walking through the door, stopping for a moment to face Ellie. "Are you sure you're up to this?"

What she wasn't up to had nothing to do with this walk, and she wasn't sure she could even define it. Or wanted to. But being so physically close to Matt—well, she'd felt that way before, which was why she was here now. Only this time there was an added bonus. She was getting to know him.

It was probably a good thing her mother had taught her that a competent woman didn't need a man because in knowing him, even a little, she was beginning to see just how wrong her mother was. Which allayed many of her fears that she was too much like her mother. She wasn't. Realizing that, she took the deepest breath of relief she'd ever had. *She was not her mother.* Ellie needed...the things her mother had told her she never would.

"Point me in the right direction, and I'll beat you there," she said, feeling like she could explode, she was so relieved. Yet taking care not to brush up against him. Because, even in her condition, she was getting a little goose-bumpy being so close.

"Up the path, then curve to the left. Follow that until you come to the divide and stay left there until you come to the big flat rock. You won't miss it because it blocks the path and to keep going up, you have to climb over it."

"But we're not climbing?" she asked.

"Nope. The rock is our destination. When you get

past it the landscape gets too rough for a woman in your condition."

He laughed, and Ellie almost melted at the deep throatiness of it as she sat down on a little rock to rest for a moment.

Matt stopped at her side, sat down with her, and took her hand. And that's when her goose-bumps rioted.

"Hell, it gets challenging to me" he continued, "and I've got some pretty good experience in rock climbing."

"Sounds like it could be fun," she said, trying to ignore the feelings coming over her. Maybe it was the air or another swing of hormones, but she felt...flushed. And in the good kind of way. From excitement or happiness. Or maybe because Matt was holding her hand. "Maybe I'll try to learn some time." She hoped to hear him offer to teach her, but he didn't. Instead, he dropped her hand, sprang up and went dashing off after Lucas, who had decided to toddle his way on up the path ahead of him. "Well, so much for that," she whispered to her baby, then likewise stood up and toddled on.

"So much for what?" he asked from ahead of her.

"Rest time," she lied. "We've got one very anxious little boy who wants to keep going."

"Well, he's not going far because our destination is only about a hundred yards from here." He stopped and held out his hand to take hers. "Need me to carry you?"

Simply sweeping her up into his arms would have been nicer, like he'd done in his office, but an extended hand was nice, too. So she took it, not sure if he was extending friendship or more. Somehow she wanted more. "Maybe on the way back down," she said.

* * *

"Were you ever married, Matt?" Ellie asked abruptly, midway through the fruit salad he'd prepared.

Her question came out of the blue and nearly choked him. "Why?" he sputtered.

"Just curious, that's all."

She'd been quiet for a while. He'd assumed it was because the walk had worn her out. But now he wasn't sure. "Never really had much interest in it. I did have a short-term thing when I was in medical school, but what we both realized was that I wasn't committed enough to the relationship, and she wasn't patient enough to deal with me. It took us about a year to come to that conclusion, and no hearts were broken when we both walked away from it."

"Did you keep yourself apart from her?" She reached for a stalk of celery to dip in the guacamole. "The way you try to do with, well, everybody."

"Do I?"

"I haven't been here that long, but I don't get the sense that you want to fit in."

He didn't, because he wasn't going to stay. So what was the point? Matt had tried fitting in the first time he'd lived here. Had tried hard. Got ridiculed or ignored. Even by social workers who were too overburdened to see what had really been going on in his family. He and Janice had gone to school. They had been clean. And had been fed—not often by their father, but fed nonetheless.

On paper, it looked fine. In reality it had been horrible. And the worst part—no one had listened. Matt had just been the kid who'd lived in the dump no one bothered with. So shutting them out before they shut him out—it was his habit. Had been as a kid, in many ways it still was. Which was why he liked being a battlefield surgeon. The noise was too loud, the need too great, and no one shut him out.

"In a lot of ways I don't. Life has never worked out for me except in the military, and that's the world in which I'm accepted. I'm good there, and I don't need anything else." Brave words that he wasn't sure he believed so much anymore. Especially with these feelings of wanting Ellie to stay. He'd come close to asking. But if she agreed, then what? How could he adjust his life to that, and would it be fair to expect her to adjust?

It was a nice thought, though. But one he couldn't let out because she was so vulnerable right now and he was afraid he could tip her in a direction she'd regret later.

"Have you ever wanted something different? Or tried to get it?"

"To what end?

"I don't know. Maybe to see if there's something bigger and better you're missing."

"Have you ever tried?" he asked.

"One night, in Reno," Ellie said, then turned her attention to the salsa and chips. "That turned into two."

Matt was dumbstruck. He didn't know what to say. Because those Reno nights had been his own stepping away from what he had been. "Why all the questions?" Matt finally asked, as he sat down next to Ellie but in a position to keep an eye on Lucas. "I don't mind telling you about me because there's not much to tell. But why are you interested?"

"Maybe because we share a baby. Or because I want to get to know the man I let my guard down for. I don't do what we did, Matt. That's not me. I don't need a man in my life, and I've done well on my own without one. But, like it or not, for a little while you're in my life, and I want to know who you are. So far, you haven't been very forthcoming."

"Because you *still* think I should be the one to raise the baby?"

"Well, I guess that's a subject for debate now that I'm gaining some insight into you. At first, you were my plan. My only plan. But now—let's just say I'm not going to pressure you about any of this. What you do is your decision, and I have too much respect for you to try and change it."

"What about your backup plan? You've got one now, don't you?

Ellie shook her head, then smiled. "Normally, my first plan works, so I rarely ever have to resort to a backup plan.

"So why not you as your backup plan? Why don't you want the responsibility of raising the baby?"

Ellie's smile disappeared, replaced by a deep scowl. "Because the women in my family don't do it well. We're not…maternal. Because I know what I'm good at and—" She felt the baby kick, and was still amazed by the feel of it. The first kick she kept to herself, but on the second kick she reached for Matt's hand and placed it on her belly.

"Whoever's in there, kicking, needs better than I'd ever be able to do. I've got money, but it's not money a baby needs. A baby, or even a growing child, needs time and attention. He or she needs to have someone to count on every minute of every day. Someone to guide and protect him. Or her. Someone to be an example. I've spent a lifetime thinking I had to turn out to be like my mother, which I know now isn't the case. But what I also know is I don't have the broader picture I need to be a good mother. There's more to it than simply being where you need to be and doing what you need to do. That's not in me."

"Are you sure? Because where you need to be is right here, right now. And as far as doing what you need to do, you're doing everything possible to take care of your pregnancy. To me, that's perfect mothering." He left his hand on her belly for a moment, then pulled it back when the kicking stopped. "Are you sure you're totally set on your decision to give up our baby?"

"Right now, I'm not set on anything. Things are changing. I'm changing. All I know is I don't want to keep the baby and raise it with surrogates, the way I was raised and the way my mother was raised. A child should have a real home. One with a parent or two parents who put that child first. I can't do that, Matt. I may have the intellectual skills to see what a baby needs but I don't have the maternal ones."

Yet there she sat with her hand on her belly, a very protective gesture. And a very maternal one. "For what it's worth, Ellie, I think you're wrong," he said, taking a bite of the guacamole, and handing a small piece of chicken to Lucas, who gobbled it right down.

"You don't know me well enough to say that."

"In surgery, I make snap decisions that deal with life-and-death circumstances, and I'm damned good at it. I made a snap decision about you in Reno, and for what we had there, I was right about it. I'm right now as well. Maybe you don't see it, but I do."

"Think what you want, Matt. I can't stop you. And I probably can't convince you you're the one who's wrong. But the man I spent those two days with in Reno—he seemed like the type who would want to be involved. And that's why I'm here."

"I *am* the type who would want to be involved, and I'm glad you included me in this. But I can't be involved in the way you think I should be." He handed another piece of chicken to Lucas, then scooted in closer to roll the toy truck to him. "I don't belong in Forgeburn anymore. I barely got out of here when I was a kid, and I don't want to be back. Don't want to limit myself to what I would have been limited to if I hadn't gotten out."

"Then go someplace else. It's a big, beautiful world out there, and most of it's *not* a battlefield."

"Right now, I can't go someplace else. I have to stay here because Child Services are trying to find—" He looked at Lucas, then lowered his voice. "A good placement. I can't mess that up for him."

"And you don't consider yourself a good placement?" she asked.

"Not at all. Not for Lucas, not for our baby. You've got to understand, Ellie, I have a commitment. I've dedicated my life to it and I have no intention of looking for some way out of it. It's who I am. Nothing about that is going to change."

"You're so sure of that?" Ellie asked. She knew he was and maybe, for the first time, she understood what it meant to have that kind of dedication. Sure, she was dedicated to her work. But her work was ever-changing, possibly to suit her restlessness. And she was restless. Always had been. Nothing ever fit.

Nothing had ever seemed right, so she'd quit being a nurse and started being a medical illustrator. Added videography when the restlessness hit again, then photography. Taken on worldwide clients, run to Tokyo for a couple of months, then London for a while. There was always something driving her to do more, be more. But it was never enough. And here was Matt, a man who simply wanted one thing—to get back to his real calling.

It dawned on her that's what she lacked—a real calling. So how could she be responsible enough to raise a baby when she didn't even know where she was going?

But how could she expect Matt to give up his calling when he knew where he needed to be in life?

"As sure as you are that your life isn't going to change."

The problem was she wasn't sure. Her life had always been plagued with doubts about how she measured up, and nothing about that had changed. Even now, sitting here with Matt, she knew she didn't even come close to measuring up to him. He was a man who did great things and aspired to do even more. And she was a woman who aspired to what? A good plan? Living up to what her mother expected? Even the thought of that made her stomach churn. But it couldn't be denied. While she wasn't like her mother, the influence was still there, holding on for dear life.

You really don't want to raise this baby, do you, Eleanor? You're starting to succeed in life, and a baby won't fit your plans.

It always got back to that, didn't it? What would fit into her plans.

You need a plan, Eleanor. Always make sure you have a plan.

But right now she didn't. "Then we have a big decision to make, don't we?" she said, feeling crushed.

"Actually, right now we have a lot of food to eat. And

I've got to finish feeding a toddler who's going to be asleep before the sun goes all the way down."

The setting sun. As beautiful as it was this early evening, and it was stunning, all she could see looked dismal. Dismal sun, dismal rocks, dismal everything. And right now the only thing Ellie wanted was to return to the *casita*, shut her doors and cry because she was desperately confused.

Matt was so unprepared for this. All of it. Lucas. Ellie. The baby. None of it fit in, yet it seemed to be taking shape right before him, and he didn't know what to do about it, especially since Lucas was becoming attached to him. Ellie had expectations, too. He knew that, and being around her, knowing what they were, made it tough on him. He cared for her. No denying that. And their baby—his feelings for *their* child were getting stronger by the minute. At first he had felt distanced from the whole thing. Knew it intellectually, but not so much emotionally.

Yet every time he looked at Ellie, strange new emotions welled up in him. Emotions he didn't understand. Not for her. Not for their baby. Could it be he wanted something he didn't yet understand? Something more than what he already had?

Matt shut his eyes for a moment and tried to picture the four of them as a typical family. Surprisingly, the image came together so easily he blinked it away before it could sink in. No, he wasn't his old man, who couldn't hack it in that sort of life. That wasn't his fear. But being responsible for someone else or, in this case, three others wasn't in his make-up, and he'd proved that with Janice. And that had been such a simple thing. He'd been supposed to get her out of Forgeburn. That's all there was to it. Get her away from there. But he hadn't, and while there might have been justified excuses, he didn't accept them. So how the hell could he take care of three people when he'd already proved he couldn't take care of one?

Yet the more Matt tried surrounding himself with thoughts of returning to his army life, the only sure thing he'd ever had, the more they eluded him, being replaced by thoughts, even visions of him being needed elsewhere now. But life, for him, wasn't an easy thing to change. He didn't do well with detours and diversions because to climb out of the hole where he'd spent his childhood had taken a straightforward progression, no veering off anywhere. And he'd trained himself in that kind of rigid discipline. Had worked hard to achieve it, then lived it every day.

But now this was all about veering off, and it felt like he was so far off he might never get back to where he had been. And there was no straightforward progression here. Not with a toddler who needed more than he could give. And a woman who didn't know what she needed who was also carrying his baby. So, no, he wasn't prepared for this. Wasn't equipped for it either. But he also couldn't turn his back on any of it because, like it or not, this was all a part of his life. Maybe not life the he'd chosen for himself but definitely the life that was being chosen for him.

So why had he called Doc Granger simply to enquire how much buying out the practice and properties would cost? Was he really thinking in that direction, or had that been a moment of weakness? Truthfully, Matt didn't know. Didn't want to think about it either.

"Want more chicken, Lucas?" he called out as the confusion of his life swirled around in his head.

Lucas, who was fully engaged in playing "hands off the teddy bear" with Ellie, looked over at Matt but didn't reply. Matt took that to mean no, so he sealed the container of food and placed it back in the backpack.

"You want something else, Ellie?" he asked. What he really wanted was to start walking and not stop until he was back where he belonged. Except this was where he belonged right now. Right here, right now, doing exactly what he was doing. Duty-bound in a direction he could have never predicted. But was it really that bad? Or was he making it worse than it seemed because it scared him how easily he slipped into the flow of it?

"I'm good, thank you," she said, smiling over at him. "But I think Lucas might need a..." she grimaced "... diaper change. Do you have one in the backpack?"

"Sure do. We're into the pull-up kind these days."

"Ah, yes. The intermediate stage. So the battlefield surgeon is an expert on toilet training?" she asked, laughing as she took the diaper from him.

He chuckled. "No, but I'm learning. And I can do that," he went on. "Lucas and I have a system."

"Oh, I think we can manage. I used to be a nurse, you know."

"Probably a very good one."

"I got along."

And she did quite brilliantly with Lucas. In fact, it was amazing, watching the way he took to Ellie. Normally, he shied away from people. But for the last twenty minutes he'd been playing with her in a way Matt had never seen. And laughing. So far, he'd never coaxed much of a laugh from Lucas, but Ellie had, and he was a little jealous of that. Jealous of a natural ability with children she couldn't see. Or didn't want to see.

She needed to keep their baby, he suddenly realized. Until now, he'd believed her when she'd said she wouldn't make a good mother. But he didn't anymore and he wondered why, with the amount of maternal instinct she was showing with Lucas, Ellie didn't want to be a mother to her own child. To their child? What kind of fear did she hide that prevented her from seeing what he was seeing right now? And it did have to be a deep fear because, when Ellie let herself go, she was a natural.

It was his intention to persuade her to keep the baby, but first he needed to discover more about why she didn't want that. Maybe, after that, help her overcome it, or simply see in herself what he was seeing. "But you said it wasn't enough."

"Nothing ever has been. I have some pretty high standards to compete with, and it seems like every time I'm about to get there, the bar rises on me a little bit more."

"Why?" he asked.

"That's the way the women in my family are. Always upward."

"But what happens if you get to the place where you're happy and contented and don't want to leave?"

"That's just it. You never do. There's always something more. Something else to achieve. Ask my mother. Ask my grandmother. They'll both tell you that contentment is the same thing as laziness."

"But do you believe that?"

"What I believe is that I'm doing what I was born to do."

This was interesting. And insightful. No matter how

good she was, where she was, it wasn't good enough. He did understand what it felt like not being good enough, but not like this. Or maybe it was all the same, just in a different version. "As in running this company you own? That's what you were born to do? Or is that just another stop-over until you find the *next* real thing?"

"You may think you're being clever, but you're not. I love what I do. But I could do more. Expand operations. Open more divisions. Go after bigger clients. Do something more in the technology line. There are a lot of opportunities out there, and I have to decide which ones are right for me because, yes, it's all about the next real thing."

"Is that *your* wish, Ellie? Or are you trying to live up to those other women in your family? You know, always upward?"

She hesitated to answer him, and Matt wished he could see the expression on her face, but it was too dark now and all he could see was her silhouette. A beautiful silhouette caught in the shadows. One he wanted to pull into his arms and simply hold because she seemed so vulnerable right now. No, she wasn't the staunch businesswoman at this moment. She was simply Ellie, and from the slump of her shoulders he could see a different person altogether. One who didn't have her plan to hide behind. One who was unsure.

"I suppose that *is* me," she finally said, after a long, deep sigh. "You know, like they say: the apple doesn't fall far from the tree."

"But what happens if you do?" he asked. "What happens if you see a better tree?"

"I did once, a long time ago. But I wasn't prepared to stay there because all I knew was what it had taught me. Unfortunately, life hadn't taught me to be independent somewhere else. In fact, all life had taught me was to grow where I was planted, so ultimately that's what I did. I didn't have experience outside of being who I was taught to be. And I was so carefully taught, I couldn't see past any of that.

"That's why I left nursing. It was my one attempt to find that better tree, but I didn't have the confidence I needed to stay there. I loved what I was doing, but I was also afraid of it, afraid of the mistakes I could make. There's no place in obstetric nursing for that kind of fear, so I went back to where my only true confidence was—the world my mother had prepared me for.

"I know my weaknesses, Matt, and I also know my strengths. For me, I find safety in my strengths, so I stay where I'm safe—as a woman who runs a growing business and knows her place there. No uncertainties, no lack of confidence. Anyway, I'm getting tired. Do you mind if we go back to the house?"

Sighing, Matt leaned back against a boulder and focused his attention on the valley below. It was too dark to see all the way to the bottom now. Kind of like his life. Too dark to see all the way to a resolution. But if he stayed here all night, morning light would bring a different view of the valley. A total view. One with new and different possibilities. If only he could share that with Ellie then maybe she, too, could see different possibilities for herself as well. And not just with the baby but with her whole life. To have so much, but to feel so small in its midst—he ached for her.

"It was a nice day," Ellie said, standing in the doorway of Lucas's bedroom while Matt put the boy to bed.

"Different from what I normally do, and I enjoyed it. Thank you."

"You're not too tired or feeling any kind of…problem, are you?"

She smiled as he pulled the blanket up over Lucas and gave the sleeping boy a kiss on the forehead. "Spoken like a typical man. All your medical training aside, pregnancy is a normal condition. It has its rough patches since the body is constantly changing, but it's been happening since the beginning of time. I'm tired, which is to be expected, but other than that there's nothing to worry about." She watched him tuck Lucas's toys into the closet then take one last look at the child before he headed for the door.

Stepping aside to let Matt pass by, Ellie looked up at him as he pressed her back into the doorframe, then stopped and stood there, looking down at her. Was he going to kiss her? She wanted him to. Wanted to feel the tenderness he'd shown her in Reno, but instead of a kiss he simply brushed his hand across her cheek. It caused her breath to catch, though. And her pulse to quicken. All too soon he stepped out of the doorway and cleared his throat. "I think I'm going to turn in early tonight," he said, as he headed down the stairs. "Is there anything I can get you before I lock up?"

It was a dismissal. She knew that, knew the sting of a slap when it hit her. "No, I'm fine. Do you mind if I use your desk for a little while? I've got my laptop and I thought maybe I could catch up on some work." Her safety net. It protected her from everything, including the hurt feelings that were welling up in her for absolutely no reason. Because there was no reason to expect Matt would be comfortable with anything other than what they were—a two-night stand with consequences. Intimacy in any form simply wasn't on the table now, and he'd been making that clear since she'd arrived. Of course, she'd been doing the same, while hoping for something different, hadn't she? Why kid herself when romance had never been a part of their relationship?

Was it the hormonal thing again? Or was she developing different feelings for Matt? She wanted it to be the hormones, but she wasn't convinced. Being away from the *old* her, even for this short amount of time, was causing something to stir inside her. Something she'd put off, or never admitted that she wanted. In her other life, why bother? It was all cut and dried. But here, in this one—well, she didn't know. She just didn't know.

"Sure. Whatever you need. Internet connection is spotty, but it usually works. So help yourself."

Ellie watched Matt lock the front door then skirt her, taking care to stay as far away from her as possible as he crossed back through to check the patio door. "Fine. I'll just go get..." She took two steps backwards then turned and retreated down the hall to the *casita*, without looking back or saying another word. What was there to say after all? That she might be falling a little in love with him? That maybe the desires she'd always kept locked away weren't as locked tight as she'd thought?

She'd never had romance in her life—not until Reno. And Matt had romanced her. Treated her the way no one else ever had. Champagne, candlelight, soft music... Considering her first in everything they'd done. So, was that what she wanted? More romance from the only man who'd ever romanced her? Or did she want even more?

Instead of gathering up her laptop to work, Ellie took a quick shower and did what everybody else in the house was doing. She went to bed and hoped for fast, deep sleep. Because she didn't want to think about Matt. And being awake, that's all she could think about. Not in the practical ways she'd taught herself to do, however. But in ways that made her want Reno back.

"I sent it off with the local helicopter pilot so now we wait." Matt was referring to the tests to determine Ellie's relaxin levels. So far, she hadn't seemed anxious to leave Forgeburn, so he wasn't pressing her to do that, or anything else. They'd spent the early part of the morning simply coexisting. Not speaking much but getting along. She'd spent a good portion of her time online, working on her business while he'd got Lucas ready for the day.

Last night he'd wanted to kiss her, and he'd thought she might be receptive. At least, to him it had seemed that way. But what would that start? Another direction he couldn't go? Damn, what was he doing, letting himself get so tempted, knowing that even if he did step over the line, he could only take that single step and no more.

Was that fair to Ellie? Or even to himself? No. It wasn't. He was obligated to a life that had no place for domesticity or romance, and even thinking he could mix those with something else was risky because his focus had always been singular. So how could he get involved with Ellie and offer her something he didn't have to offer?

So many consequences from one little kiss that hadn't happened. But consequences be damned. Matt wished he'd gone ahead and done it anyway. Well, he hadn't, and there was really no reason to speculate about what might have happened. He'd had his chance, hadn't taken it and the rest was an empty point.

Matt wasn't like his old man, who'd shirked every responsibility life had given him. He knew that. But he'd gone to the opposite extreme, there really wasn't any give in him. It was black, or it was white. There was nothing in between because in the in between that's where he found his doubts and fears, and the terrifying nightmare that one bad move and he'd end up right back here, not as the doctor but as the kid who lived in the dump. It terrified him, thinking how easy it could be to take that one wrong step.

It terrified him even more thinking that Ellie could be dragged into all that with him. Some might look at her as his way out, but he would never use her that way. And while she could offer him a part of life he'd never had, he could do the same. Only what she would offer would be good for him and what he'd offer would be bad for her. Which was why Matt kept to the straight and narrow.

Ellie deserved better, so did Lucas, the baby certainly deserved better than the mire he'd never quite escaped. Even with glimpses of what he could have if he took that one step off the path, it wasn't enough to budge him. Not for his sake and especially not for theirs.

Yet, in the distance, he could still see a different life. Unfortunately, he was so stuck where he was, Matt didn't know how to reach out and grab it. A simple kiss might have been the start. Or it might have been the stumble that started him on the descent. Which was why he hadn't kissed her. He had been afraid where it would take him. And, most of all, take Ellie.

"I appreciate that," Ellie said, without diverting

her attention from her computer screen. "I'd feel better knowing what I'm dealing with before I make that long trip back. That is, if you don't mind my staying for an extra couple of days." She looked up at him for an answer but her face was impassive. No expression. "Or I could stay in that hotel down the road. That was always my first option."

"The *casita* is fine," Matt said, picking up his medical bag. "Look, I've got some patients coming into the office in a while. I'm also going to keep Lucas with me this morning because the social worker has some prospective parents, and they're going to stop in for a few minutes. If you'd like to come with us, you're welcome. I have better connectivity at the office than I do here, so you might have an easier time working there."

She looked up, her face almost registering alarm. "They might want to adopt him?"

"That's always been the plan."

"But I thought…"

"What, Ellie? That this little slice of domesticity we're living might rub off?"

"Maybe—I don't know. Hearing you talk about it then seeing it actually happen—I guess I wasn't prepared for that."

Matt shook his head. "Sometimes reality bites, but my reality is a battlefield hospital full of casualties that need to be fixed. You've always known that."

"Just make sure you don't turn yourself into a casualty as well," Ellie said. "And I don't mean battlefield."

Then, just like that, she turned him off and launched into an internet conversation with a colleague.

Matt took his cue, held out his hand for Lucas, who grabbed it, and headed out the door. By the time the two of them reached the truck, Matt was kicking himself for not trying harder to get her to go with him. He didn't like leaving Ellie alone, even when she insisted she was fine. Maybe it was an overprotective reaction to her pregnancy, maybe it was about some different feelings for her stirring up in him.

Whatever the case, she'd made her choice, and he had to get over the idea that he was responsible for her. He wasn't, and she'd made it perfectly clear that's the way she intended to keep it. So, had her grumpiness this morning just been a by-product of anxiety over missing work? Something to do with her pregnancy? Or the kiss that had never happened? Had she wanted it badly enough she was still brooding over it?

Was she expecting kisses like they'd shared in Reno?

Which meant… He swallowed hard. "Well, Lucas, it looks like it's just the two of us today. You up for being my receptionist in the office?"

Of course, Lucas didn't respond. But Matt did notice that the boy was staring more intently at him than he usually did. Eyes open a little wider than normal. Expression a little more animated. Which was oddly discomforting. He loved this kid. It hadn't taken much, but he totally, hopelessly loved this kid, and what he was about to do… "Apparently," he said, as he strapped him to the infant seat in the truck, "one of us looks like he's going to have a good day." And the other one was already dreading the rest of it.

CHAPTER SIX

"MR. AND MRS. RIGSBY. They're outside. They'd like to have a look at Lucas."

Matt glanced up from his desk at Lucas's social worker, Mary Jane Snider, as trepidation knotted his stomach. Sure, this is what he'd asked for, but now that it was so close he wasn't as set on adoption as he'd been initially. But Lucas needed more than he could offer. And he owed it to Janice to see that Lucas got the very best. God knew, he'd failed his sister in doing that for her. And being a child, trying to raise a child, wasn't an excuse. To some maybe. But not to him. His sister had been his responsibility from the time he'd been five and she three, and that was the one responsibility in life he'd failed. He wasn't going to fail Lucas, though. "Good," he said half-heartedly. "Show them in."

He stood, went to the Dutch door play area connected to his office, and reached over for Lucas, who stood there with his arms up, smiling, waiting to be picked up. "Don't be afraid of all the people," he told the boy. "They want to be your friends." Try as he might, he could raise no enthusiasm in his voice.

"Remember me?" Mary Jane said, stepping forward to take Lucas from Matt.

Lucas's response was to draw harder into Matt's shoulder and bury his face. "He's not good with strangers yet," Matt explained. "It takes him a while to warm up to them."

"Any chance he'll warm up by the time I bring the Rigsbys in?" she asked, stepping back.

"Probably not."

"We could schedule for another time. Maybe by next week…"

Matt shook his head. "This is who he is. If they're interested in him, they'll have to accept it."

Mary Jane nodded, left the office, then returned a minute later with the Rigsbys—Mr. Rigsby with his hands stuffed into the pockets of a pinstriped suit, something no one out here wore, and Mrs. Rigsby with her arms folded across her chest. Neither looked unfriendly, though. Just indifferent. And older than he'd thought they would be. He doubted Mr. Rigsby would be able to teach Lucas how to climb a rock when the time came, due to his age. And Mrs. Rigsby—she seemed too nervous. Or out of place. Could someone like that nurture Lucas the way he'd need to be nurtured?

"This is Lucas," he said, making no attempt to get Lucas to look at them. "He's shy," he explained.

"Does he walk?" Mr. Rigsby asked.

"Yes, he does. But he doesn't talk, yet."

"Is he slow?" Mrs. Rigsby asked. "Is that why he doesn't talk?"

"He doesn't talk because he has nothing to say. And, no, he's not slow. More like he's just taking life at his own pace."

"Does his pace include toilet training?" Mr. Rigsby enquired.

"Not yet, but we're working on it."

"Any peculiar habits?" Mr. Rigsby continued.

"What do you mean by peculiar? He's two. Most of his habits could be described as peculiar."

"Just oddities," the man said. "Things you wouldn't normally expect to see a toddler doing."

Matt had no idea what other toddlers this age did, but nothing Lucas did seemed odd or peculiar to him. Actually, he suspected that hiding under that shy exterior was a bright little boy. The signs were there. Just not ready to bloom yet. "He has a pet skink he likes to play with in the rock garden," Matt said.

"A skink?" Mrs. Rigsby asked, shuddering.

"Lizard. Brown body, blue tail."

"The child has a skink?" Mr. Rigsby said.

Matt nodded.

"Well, that skink won't be coming with us if we decide to take Lucas in," Mrs. Rigsby said. "We don't have pets in the house, and the people who work for us—"

"People?" Matt interrupted.

"Well, right now we have a cook and a housekeeper. With Lucas coming in, of course we'd hire a tutor and a nanny."

Another time, another place, this might have sounded like a good idea. But he knew that was how Ellie had been raised, and saw the conflicts in her because of it. Certainly, the Rigsbys would be different from Ellie's mother but, still, the similarities—this wasn't what Lucas needed. None of it. What he needed was what neither Matt nor Ellie had had—people who would love raising him.

"I'm sorry," Matt asked. "But I'd hoped to place him

with a family who was going to be personally involved with him."

"Which is exactly what we intend to do, Doctor," Mr. Rigsby said, his patience obviously brittle now.

"With hired help?"

"Because we only want the boy to have the best," Mrs. Rigsby said.

But what they offered wasn't the best. Maybe they couldn't see it, but he could, thanks to Ellie. "So do I," Matt said, taking Lucas back to his play area. "I'm sorry for wasting your time."

He went inside, shut the door, and sat down on the rug with Lucas to help him stack green and purple and red wooden blocks. This wasn't what he'd expected. In his mind, the adopting couple would have been eager and excited, full of wonderful plans for Lucas, anxious to bond as a family. Maybe even gushing over him a little bit. Maybe he was simply being too picky, but that was an ideal Matt had always had for himself when he'd been young. A real family, with eager, excited parents who were full of wonderful plans for him and Janice. Parents who were anxious to bond as a family.

He'd never had it, which was why he wanted it for Lucas. But Lucas would get it. He would see to that, no matter how many people he had to turn down to get to the right ones.

"Are you sure you know what you're doing? I could call them back…" Mary Jane said, leaning over the Dutch door.

"Yes. For a change, I really am sure."

It was well into the night when Matt finally dragged himself through the front door. Betty Nelson had come to get Lucas when he'd called her. He might have asked Ellie, but he hadn't had time to take Lucas home, and he certainly hadn't wanted Ellie making that drive until he was sure of her condition. So, after he'd called Ellie and told her he had an emergency, he'd called Betty, and she'd been there with open arms for Lucas in the blink of an eye.

He was blessed to have her as Lucas's babysitter. And Lucas did respond well to her. But, then, back in the day, when she'd been his teacher, she'd always been there for him, too, and she'd become one of the few examples in his life who'd shown him that there were good people in the world. Something he hadn't really experienced very much.

"Bad one?" Ellie asked, waiting for him just inside the door with a glass of fruit drink she'd made.

"Sorry I'm so late," he said, taking the glass she offered him, then heading for the big easy chair in front of the fireplace in the living room. "Not bad as much as it was tedious. One of the resort guests stepped over the safety fence to take a better picture and fell down a cliff. Not a huge one, thank God, but he busted his head open, and I had to help go down and get him.

"The local rangers weren't available to help, so it took me almost an hour to get the equipment I needed, then get to him, and another hour to stabilize him enough to get him back up. The first half of it wasn't so bad because he was unconscious, but when he started to come to, he wasn't very coherent, but he was *very* combative. With some help from the resort staff, we finally got him stabilized enough, and secured enough, to get him into an air rescue chopper."

Without thinking, Matt rubbed his jaw, then worked

it back and forth. "I flew in with him to make sure he didn't get worse, which he didn't. But he's going to need surgery. The good news is he should be OK. The bad news is I feel like I've been put through hell."

"He hit you?" Ellie asked, bending to look at his jaw. She cupped his head in her hand and turned it gently. "You're already bruising."

"I've had worse," he said, leaning his head back in the chair, closing his eyes, drawing in a deep breath and wincing.

"Where else are you hurt, Matt?" she asked. "And do you want me to go get Lucas?"

Matt shook his head. "I talked to Betty a few minutes ago, and she said he's already asleep for the night. She doesn't have a problem letting him stay there and, to be honest, with the way I'm feeling I really don't think I'd be very good for him to be around tonight." He tried to resituate in the chair and winced again.

"Shirt off, Matt," Ellie said.

"Sorry, not in the mood for *that*," he said, attempting as much of a grin as his sore jaw would allow.

"No joking around here. Take your shirt off. I want to see what's going on."

It was nice having someone care for him for a change. Usually it was the other way around. In fact, in his entire life he couldn't remember a time when someone else had ever offered to take care of him in any way. And while this was only Ellie getting ready to plunge into nurse mode, he was touched. "Not sure I can lean forward enough to do that, and I don't want to stand up. I'll be fine, but I appreciate the concern."

"And in the morning? When you have to function again? What happens then?"

"I do it without trying to groan too loudly."

"Shirt off, cowboy," she said, her voice unusually soft as she leaned over to unbutton it.

Truth was, Matt didn't want to see the damage because he feared he might have a couple of cracked ribs. So he shut his eyes as she exposed his chest, then held his breath as she ran her fingers lightly over it, fighting back the urges that had overtaken him so quickly with her before.

She'd laughed that night when she'd seen what she had caused, and so fast, then had shifted her attention to far better areas while he'd lain there, helpless to do anything but enjoy. And watch her. Loving everything he'd seen. And it wasn't like he was a starving man sexually. There had been times overseas... But her touch—it had aroused him so quickly he'd almost been embarrassed by his lack of stamina.

Yes, he remembered it well. Had thought about it too many times since Reno, because no other woman had ever caused that kind of response in him. Like the shiver that was running up and down his back right now. And the memories of her beautiful body atop his, underneath his. But he was fighting all that. Or, at least, trying to. So why not simply let it happen again? What would happen if he did?

For starters, he wouldn't be able to walk away from it this time. Because now Ellie came with commitments. And even though her touch caused thoughts of the two of them together, he had no right to think that. Still, in Reno, that touch had also compelled him to see her a second night when he'd vowed not to—the night when she must have gotten pregnant as his condom had...slipped. He'd told her, of course, but she hadn't been worried because it hadn't been her fertile time of the month.

Yet her touch had caused a big consequence from something that was meant to be transient, simply because he'd been unable to resist her. Was that what would happen again if he gave in to what he was feeling? Another big consequence? "Damn, that hurts," he choked, as she probed a little harder.

"Well, without a way to get you X-rayed, I can't say for sure, but I'm not feeling anything that would indicate your ribs are broken. In fact, the bruising is a little lower than your rib cage, so the concern would be more about internal bleeding."

Even though Ellie wasn't feeling anything seriously wrong, Matt was, and it had nothing to do with his present physical condition and everything to do with the *what ifs* and *why nots* running through his mind. "Comforting thought," he muttered, finally looking down at himself. "He kicked me."

"Apparently. And more than once. How'd you let that happen?" she asked, while probing his rock-hard abdomen to see if she could detect any internal bleeding.

"He wasn't conscious. Then he was, and he was disoriented."

"Well, I'm not feeling anything distended so I don't think you've got a bleed going on. Where's your medical bag?"

"On the chair by the door. But you don't need to—" Too late. She was already off to get it, and he sensed a complete physical coming up. "I'm really OK," he shouted after her.

"You're really not," she said, coming back over to him, his stethoscope already out of the bag. "So we either do this upstairs in your bed, if you're up to climbing the stairs, or in the *casita*, since it's on this level. Your choice."

"What if my choice is to sit here, drink the rest of the fruit juice, then take a nap?"

"You can, but I'm still going to examine you, and if I have to do it while you're in the chair…" She pointed to her lower back, then smiled. "Don't give another thought to the idea that it could cause me back pain."

Matt chuckled at Ellie's attempt to blackmail him. It was cute. "OK, you win. You can play doctor."

"How about I simply *be* a nurse?"

He sighed, then pushed himself to the edge of the chair, realizing he hurt more now that he had only a little while ago. Ellie extended a hand to help him up, and he was grateful for it, both physically and emotionally. "I've been on the battlefield for almost two years in total, and nothing that's ever happened there comes close to what happened here," he said as he stood. "I think I'm getting soft."

Ellie laughed as she put a steadying arm around his waist. "Just felt your abs. Trust me, you're not getting soft. At least, not since Reno. Now, how about we just skip the stairs and go to the *casita*?"

"Sounds like a plan," he said, trying not to put any weight on her. She was, after all, pregnant. But tough. He liked that. Hadn't seen it before in the women he'd known, but this was one tough lady.

As they walked down the hall, Matt wondered what it would be like to have Ellie there all the time. It couldn't happen, of course. Neither of their lives would allow it. But the dream was nice. Cozy little family. Coming home to Ellie of an evening, and the two of them talking, or the four of them picnicking up on the flats. Lazy Sunday mornings, sleeping late—until the kids woke them up with their own plans for the day. Family meals. Yes, a nice dream, but Ellie would soon be going one way and he'd be going another. So what was the point of thinking about something that would never happen? "You want my trousers off?" he asked as they entered the *casita*.

"Wouldn't hurt. And I know you're not modest." She patted her belly. "Proof's right here."

He chuckled. "Would it be too much to ask you to undress me?"

"I did that once. Look where it got us. So take off your own trousers, get yourself situated, and I'll be back in a minute to take off your boots and socks."

"Where are you going?" he asked, as he undid the button on his jeans.

"To fix an ice pack for your jaw."

Matt watched her walk away, enjoying the view. Pregnant, not pregnant, any way he looked at her Ellie was a beautiful woman. Stunning. And the baby bump she was still trying to conceal under baggy clothes made her even more beautiful. Glowing as only an expectant woman could. He hoped that somehow, as her belly swelled even more, he'd be able to see that because he wanted to watch the changes.

Or would those changes serve to remind him later on that this couldn't be his life? That melancholy thought swept over him so quickly it felt worse than the kicks he'd taken to the gut.

"Just hold this to your jaw, and it would help if you got your jeans all the way off. One button isn't quite enough."

"Boots and socks, too?" he asked, trying to force a grin, even though the heavy thoughts of the inevitable weren't letting go.

"Might be a nice picture for one of my social media accounts," she teased, as Matt, with Ellie's help, stripped down then stretched out on the bed.

"Well, whatever you do, just be gentle," he said, closing his eyes, and not because he didn't want to see her. It was because he was trying to block out thoughts and images popping into his head that didn't have a place there. Thoughts and images of a different life for him. One he'd never had. One he wasn't even sure he understood. And one that scared him worse than being under fire on the battlefield did.

Matt did have a beautiful body. It hadn't been the reason for her initial attraction in Reno, though. That would have been his smile—so warm, curving into a sensuousness Ellie couldn't take her eyes off. She'd missed that afterward. Missed waking up next to him like she had those two mornings, with that smile. Missed going to bed with him like those two evenings, with that sensual smile. Now, when he did smile, it was full of worry and she understood why, but was there a way, other than seducing him, to entice his other smile back?

Along with his smile, everything else about Matt, as a man, was perfect. She'd admired it all in Reno. Boldly, openly for him to hear, just to please him. Then he'd moved—so smooth, so self-assured. And his hands— so strong and gentle. And his patience—maybe that was what had surprised Ellie the most about him. He'd been so bold going to his room, then, suddenly, when second thoughts and shyness had overtaken her, he'd waited, hadn't rushed her, hadn't ridiculed her. For that, she had almost fallen in love with him.

Then days later, when she had been back home, back in her same old routine, her dreams had been of Matt, and now, seeing him again—Ellie sighed, trying to get hold of herself. Letting herself be seduced by the memories wasn't why she was here. Still, seeing him undressed and sprawled across the bed...the memories simply wouldn't quit, try as she may to put them out of her head. But Matt was the substance of the most powerful, potent memories she'd ever had because he was the only one who'd ever found his way into the place she'd never allowed anyone to enter.

"Well, first let me listen to your chest. Make sure nothing's rattling around in there." Ellie had her listen, was convinced he was good, then went on to his blood pressure, which was perfect, despite the circumstances. Looked in his eyes, she saw nothing there, at least no popped blood vessels even though there was some swelling around his eye now. All while trying to keep her breath steady, keep her goose-bumps at bay, keep her fingers from wandering to places they had no business being. Places she had wandered to before.

Focus, Ellie told herself as she returned to his ribs. They still worried her, since there was no way to have a look at them. Suppose one had cracked? It could cause a fluid build-up, eventually lead to a collapsed lung. And he didn't necessarily have to show symptoms for that to happen. "I'm going to listen to your chest again, then go back over your ribs. I'm afraid I might have— "

Matt held up his hand to stop her. "Is this why you left nursing? Because you second-guessed yourself?"

"There was always so much at risk."

"And you didn't have the confidence to believe you were good enough to take care of it?"

"I was good in the academic sense when I was a student, but once I was on the hospital floor it all seemed too important."

"And what you're doing now isn't important?"

"It is important, but in a different way. While I was a nurse, the decisions I made were…costly. People counted on them, and what I did affected lives. You know, life or death situations. What I do now… My decisions are important, but in a different way. I make decisions, but the outcome isn't as crucial because I have fact checkers and art editors who nit-pick everything we produce. In the hospital, there was no one to come behind me to make sure what I was doing was correct."

"Is that the way you were raised? Always in doubt of your decisions? Always with someone looking over your shoulder, nit-picking?"

"Not from the nannies and tutors. But my mother never thought I was good enough—at least, not as good as her—and she questioned everything I did or said. Always for my own good, she'd tell me. She would also tell me she was preparing me to take over her company someday, which wasn't what I wanted."

"Hence you chose nursing."

"Yeah. Medicine had never crossed my mind, but I wanted to break away from her, do something totally different with my life. Only what I chose didn't give me the confidence I lacked." Ellie sat down on the edge of the bed next to him.

"There was a baby—blue baby, actually. Not breathing. The mother was bleeding out and the whole medical team was focused on saving her. But they handed me the baby, and it was up to me to resuscitate him. I tried, Matt. I really tried. But he never did breathe. So in the end the mother lived but her baby didn't, and the look on her face when she found out… I resigned the next day because I did my best and I couldn't…"

And now he knew her deepest fear.

"Fix the situation?" he asked, reaching out to take her hand. "It happens, Ellie. There are patients we can't save. It's not easy, and sometimes it's so downright gut-wrenching that all you want to do is crawl off somewhere and cry. I know. I've been there too many times. And, yes, I've been the one who has crawled off and cried. But then there are the ones we do save. The easy saves. The hard saves. The miracles. And so many that fall in between. While they never make up for the ones we lose, the ones we save are the reason we keep trying."

"Except I didn't. I gave up. I couldn't save him and I…" She shook her head. "I couldn't go through that again."

"I know it's a harsh reality to face, and I'm sorry it happened. But you didn't give up. At least, not your compassion or your love of medicine. You simply took a different route, sort of like what I'm doing now. It all counts. The bottom line is, Ellie, not everyone is cut out for every job. You weren't cut out for obstetrics, but that doesn't mean you're not cut out to be a mother. A mother's love and a nurse's duty are two entirely different things. A mother's love will always win over everything else. Including her fears."

Not that he'd ever had a mother's love, but in his ideal world that's the way a mother should be. A perfect mother would be... Ellie. If only she could see that. And not just for the baby's sake but her own.

"Except when you fail."

"But you didn't fail, Ellie. You were presented with a situation that wouldn't have turned out any differently for anybody else. But somehow you've got the idea that you've got to be better than everybody else or you're not good enough. Which just isn't the case. I looked at some of what you do online, and you teach people, through your work, to be better doctors and nurses. You inform patients about prescriptions and health conditions. You bring understanding and caution to a very scary time in a person's life, and that's important. What you do is important, Ellie. Who you are is important, no matter what you've been brought up to believe. And as far as my ribs go, no second guesses. You were right the first time."

"Can I at least wrap them?" she said, as a stray tear slid down her cheek.

"You can wrap anything you like," he said. "Except I don't have a stretch bandage here. So it'll have to wait until morning when I open up the office."

"Just this once, indulge me. Let me go get that. I'm fine to drive, and I do want to make sure..."

He chuckled. "Keys are in my jeans. And if you're not back in thirty minutes, I'm coming to get you."

"Want me to text you every five minutes just so you'll know I'm OK?" She would have if he'd asked, even though it seemed silly. But having someone to care for her—if only for a moment—was nice.

"Just when you get there, and when you're leaving."

Matt smiled at her, and for the first time since Reno

it was the smile she'd loved at the start. A smile that made all her doubts seem insignificant.

Fifteen minutes later Ellie inserted the key in Matt's office door, went inside and turned on the light. He'd said the supplies were kept in the closet in his office so she texted him and headed straight there, determined to make this a quick trip, found what she was looking for, texted him again, then headed straight out.

On the way, though, she paused to smile at the fax machine—a very old one. Old technology—it figured. She wondered, if Matt stayed long enough, whether he would upgrade. Then she remembered several different computers, tables and such she'd put into storage in her own company after they'd upgraded. She'd intended to donate them somewhere but hadn't gotten around to it. Would Matt benefit from some of what she had? She'd ask him, because, seriously, a fax machine...

Except the fax had a sheet of paper on it. Someone had faxed him. Without thinking about it, Ellie pulled it out, intending to take it to him since it might be important, and his odds of even coming to the office tomorrow were slim. And, yes, she looked at it. Not to be nosy but simply because it was in her hand. What she saw was her name at the top, as the patient, followed by her lab results.

Ellie's first impression was that had been a mighty quick turnaround. Then curiosity got the best of her so she looked at the results. Nothing had changed much from her last lab work. Except what was printed in red, which was the lab's indicator that something was wrong. It was her relaxin number, and it was above two. Halfway to three, actually. Her hands started to shake. That was more than twice the norm. Which meant *she was in trouble*. As was her pregnancy, and her baby.

CHAPTER SEVEN

MATT WAS SLEEPING by the time Ellie got back with the bandage, and she debated disturbing him. But if, by some chance, he did have a broken rib or two, he needed to have them bandaged. So she stood in the doorway of the *casita* for a moment, watched him sleep, with the sheet pulled up to his waist now and his bare abs exposed.

And with the lab results in her pocket. She knew she should tell him right off, but now didn't seem the time to bother him with any of this. Tomorrow would be another day, and the results would keep.

"Matt," she said, crossing over to the bed, "I've got the bandage." But he didn't answer, he was sleeping so soundly. She tried again, this time giving him a little nudge on the shoulder. The ice pack had slipped off his jaw and melted into a puddle in the bed near his face. "I really need to get this thing on you."

He opened his eyes slowly, attempted to smile up at her but winced then rubbed his jaw. "I think the bed might be a little wet," he said, sliding over enough to avoid the damp area. "Meant to get up and change the ice but—"

"The only thing you need to do is co-operate with

me. I can change the bed after I've got the bandage on, then you can go back to sleep." Changing the bed with the patient still in it—one of her old nursing skills coming back. When she'd left the profession she'd had regrets but she'd never looked back. And here she was now, being a nurse again. Oddly enough, she was enjoying it more than she'd thought she would. Or maybe it was because she was taking care of Matt. "Sit up, and help me get it in place. Keep it snug, but not snug enough to hurt or do any damage."

"You've got a good bedside manner," Matt said as he struggled to help her with the bandage. Once it was in place, she slid her fingers between the bandage and his skin to make sure it wasn't too tight, and heard him gasp.

"Pain?" Ellie asked.

"Not exactly." Suddenly he reached up, pulled her face to his and kissed her. Gingerly. Tenderly. And only for a moment before he backed away from it. "Now, *that* hurt," he said, rubbing his jaw.

"Why, Matt?" she asked, stepping back from him.

"Why does it hurt?"

"No. Why did you kiss me?"

"Spur of the moment. Impulse. Giving in to being a man with a beautiful, kissable woman fussing over his body."

They weren't the words Ellie wanted to hear. Although she didn't know what she did want to hear. Maybe that he cared for her or was falling for her a little bit would have been nice. She stopped at that because anything else would have been too much wishful thinking and sad.

"That's not who we are," she said, moving back to

the bed to fasten the end of his bandage in place, yet taking care to stay as far away from him as possible. "It wasn't in Reno, and it's not now." Although the kiss had been wonderful. She remembered his kisses, remembered so many other things from those couple of days. The laughing, the talking, wrapped in the sheet dancing and a little bit drunk. So amazing. In fact, almost too amazing for the likes of two people who didn't want commitment.

"Who we are is who we want to be."

"Who we are, Matt, is a woman who will be returning to the corporate world shortly, and a man who'll be returning to the battlefield. How do you make something like that work?"

Matt reached out, took hold of her hand and pulled her over to him. "By not being so rigid that we can't enjoy the moment and accept it for what it is. *Again*. Two people who are crazy attracted to each other, who made a baby together because of that, who are simply looking for the right thing to do." He forced himself into an upright position. "It's not rocket science, Ellie. It's simply us trying to be connected to something more than we already have." He patted the bed beside him. "Do you want to be connected? And I don't mean sexually right now."

"I do," she whispered, sitting down with him, then snuggling into his arms when he pulled her there. "But I don't think I know how, because I've never really been connected to anybody before." Except her baby, and that connection was growing inside every day.

"One step at a time, Ellie. That's the best most of us can do. One step at a time." With that he pulled her down into the bed, where they lay, still snuggled together. Connected.

It had been a painful sleep, but nice, having Ellie there with him. Matt had managed to take off her shoes, but hadn't wanted to wake her up as she had been sleeping so soundly he'd known she must be exhausted, so he'd left her in her clothes, then spooned in next to her, even though it had hurt, and had listened to her gentle breathing awhile before he'd dropped off to sleep himself.

Now, if possible, he ached more than he had last night. But it was worth it, waking up while she was still asleep, still immersed in a world without worries.

Cautiously, Matt rolled over then sat on the side of the bed for a moment, trying to catch his breath, before he got up and attempted the shower. But as he rolled, so did she, pulling up the cotton shirt she wore and exposing her belly.

It was surprisingly more rounded than he'd expected, even though he'd felt it before through fabric as their baby had kicked. Round and beautiful. But now, seeing it this way, stark and naked, it was hard to imagine that his child would come from this belly. *His child.* Tears sprang to his eyes and he couldn't claim them to be hormonal the way she did. But he was touched. Truly touched and overwhelmed by something as simple as a belly bump. It happened to women every day, but this was different. Matt *was* connected, for the first time in his life.

Matt swiped back the tears and attempted to stand. But his movements woke Ellie up, and she opened her eyes and smiled at him. "I really didn't mean to sleep here," she said, to his back.

He sniffed. "Did you sleep well?"

"Better than I have since, well, I don't remember when. So, are you getting up?"

"Need a shower before I go to work."

"You're not up for a shower yet, Matt. And in your shape, you can't work."

He felt her struggle to a sitting position behind him, but still didn't turn around to look at her. His emotions were still too wobbly for that. "Life goes on, Ellie. Sore ribs or not. People depend on me and they don't particularly care that I have things going on in my life that might stop me from seeing them. When you need a doctor, you need a doctor."

"And there's no one else around you can call? A locum?"

"Easier said than done. Resources are stretched thin, and Doc Granger said that nobody likes coming out here. He'd have to make a request weeks in advance when he needed someone to cover for him. And if he needed someone in a hurry, he'd send his patient to the clinic in Whipple Creek, which is a little over a hundred miles from here. So no. There's no one to cover for me right now, and I do have patients lined up."

"Have you thought about bringing someone else in to help?"

"Technically, this isn't my practice. I'm running it, not buying it. So that decision would have to be made by Doc Granger." He gave himself a push off the bed, stopped midway to catch his breath, then finally stood. Then, and only then, did he turn around to face her, and notice her shirt was pulled back down, covering her completely. "Which means off to the shower."

"Can I help you?" she asked, starting to scoot to the edge of the bed.

Normally, he might have jumped at the chance. He could almost feel her crammed into the shower stall with him, pressed to him, the two of them separated only by a slippery film of soap. But that wasn't for today. Probably not for any day. So as quickly as he could, he started walking toward the bathroom. "Nope. No help needed. Except afterwards, when I'll need help getting back into this bandage."

"Then maybe I'll go make us some juice," she said. "And please, leave the bathroom door open so I can hear you in case you need something."

"Sure." It was a fast agreement, brought on by the fact that he was aroused again and he didn't want her to know. But this was how he'd responded to her in Reno, and he supposed she already knew this was how he was responding to her here.

The shower was difficult. More bruises were showing on his body now, and the spray of the water hurt. Everything hurt. And, as Matt discovered, getting out, drying off and getting dressed wasn't going to be easy. He was simply too stiff, too sore to move easily. But he did manage to make it back to the bed, where he sat naked, staring at nothing for what seemed an interminable amount of time, hoping his strength would return.

"Matt, you OK?" Ellie called through the *casita* door.

He wanted to say yes. Wanted to prove he was more than he really was at the moment. But in truth he wasn't going to be able to wrap the bandage again, let alone get his jeans, socks and boots on. "Good," he called back. "Getting dressed. It might take me a little while. I'm slower than I expected to be this morning."

She entered the *casita* with two fruit juices in hand, set them down and walked over to him. "How long have you been sitting there—naked?"

He looked down and realized he hadn't even bothered to cover himself with a bed sheet or towel. "Maybe ten minutes."

"And you didn't call me to help you dress?"

"Maybe I didn't want to admit I was weaker than I thought." He yanked the corner of the bed sheet across his lap.

Ellie laughed. "Men," she said, on her way back to the *casita* door. "You stay where you are, and I'll get you some clean clothes, then I'll help you get dressed. Oh, and as for the rest of your day, I'll cancel your appointments because you, Dr. McClain, get to spend the day sitting down with your feet propped up."

Matt wanted to argue, but Ellie was right. He was moved by how she observed him and how she wanted to take care of him. And saddened at the same time as he knew this connection was only temporary. They had separate ways to go, and soon.

Ellie really hadn't intended to spend the night in his arms, but it had been nice. She'd woken a couple of times and heard him breathe. Steady, strong, like she remembered from Reno. She recalled that after their first night together she'd wondered what it would be like waking up with someone like Matt every morning. In her mind, they'd be lazy about it. Linger together in bed as long as they could. Then make love. Shower together. Hate parting to go to their separate jobs.

In reality, that wasn't going to happen, of course. But Matt in his condition and she in hers—it was still nice. And now, as she went over his appointment list, making the various calls to cancel his appointments, she still couldn't shake the mellow feeling that simply sleeping with him had caused. It almost nullified the anxiousness over the lab report.

"Everything under control?" Matt asked, as he entered his home office.

"Called everybody on your list. Talked directly to three of them, left messages for two. And that ranch appointment—I did cancel that and told him you'd get back to him when you were up to the ride. I also gave him the contact information for Whipple Creek in case he wanted to make that trip."

"Which makes me a man of leisure today," he said, dropping down into the chair across from his desk. The one Lucas usually sat in. "But I do have to go get Lucas."

"Taken care of. I called Betty and she agreed to keep him this morning. I'll pick him up after lunch." She'd gotten herself busy to keep from confronting the obvious, but now was the time. She had to tell him. "Um, when I was at your clinic yesterday…" She handed him the sheet of paper with the lab results.

He studied it for a moment, then looked up at her. "Why didn't you show me this last night?"

"I was trying to come to terms with it. And you were so tired I didn't want you taking on any more than you already had to deal with. My level is over two, Matt." She sniffled. "That puts me at—"

"I know what it puts you at," he said, standing then walking around the desk and wrapping his arms around her shoulders. "It puts you at a higher than normal risk for miscarriage or premature birth because relaxin, in the later stages of pregnancy, prepares the body for childbirth. But if the body is tricked into believing the rising levels of the hormone means it's time, it's done its job and got the process started, whether the pregnancy has gone full term or not… That's the clinical aspect of it. But the personal aspect is we're going to deal with it, together."

"How," she asked him, glad for the way he held her, and stepped in to give her support like no one had ever given her before. Normally Ellie was alone in dealing with problems, but now, having someone there to help her through…

"First by getting in touch with a friend of mine who specializes in high-risk pregnancies. Unfortunately she's in California, so I think the odds of you going to see her are zero because you're not going to be able to travel that far until you've been checked. And I'm not qualified to do that. But Susie—Dr. Susan Caldwell— can get us started in the right direction."

"And in the meantime?"

"You rest. Normally, I'd prescribe a healthy diet, but you already have that. You'll probably need an ultrasound and several other tests. But no travel for now. And no work. Until we know more, I'd also like to keep you isolated as much as possible. You know, colds, flu, those sorts of things. And we'll have to find you a doctor and a hospital that's set up to do a special care delivery, if that's what it comes to."

Ellie leaned her head against his arm. "It sounds like you expect me to stay here for the duration of my pregnancy, but I can't do that, Matt."

"Why not?"

"Because it was never my intention to disrupt your life. I intended to come and go."

"Making sure you and our baby are healthy isn't a disruption, Ellie. And what happens if you go back to Reno? Is there someone there who could help you through this?

"No, but I could hire—"

"A nurse? Is that what you want? Someone paid to take care of you, or someone who truly cares taking care of you?

"But I don't want to be your burden. Especially now that there could be complications," she said, swiping at her tears with the back of her hand.

"You're having my baby, Ellie. Taking care of you is no burden. It's what I want to do—*need* to do."

"What about going back to the army? You can't stay on leave indefinitely."

"I have two months of leave saved, which I'm about to use up. There are other things I can do instead that won't affect my standing. One would be vacating my contract and serving the rest of my time as a reserve officer. Then, when that duty is over, re-enlist. As long as it's for a justified family cause, there's no reason they won't let me back in when the time comes."

"You'd do that for me?" Knowing someone would make that kind of sacrifice for her caused her tears to flow even harder. "Put aside everything you want to take care of me?"

"Of course I would. Unless you push me away, I want to stay with you through your pregnancy."

But not after. While Ellie hadn't expected Matt to make that kind of commitment, part of her had hoped for it. The pregnant part probably. So once the baby was born and the hormones were doing what they should, would she still have these feelings and longings for Matt in a way she should never have? Or would they disappear, the way he would?

Ellie hadn't meant to break down the way she had. What she'd hoped was that she'd be emotionless when telling him, and he'd be emotionless when they had a clear-headed talk about what to do. Well, the best-laid plans on that one. She'd been emotional and he'd been supportive, which made her feel even more emotional. And now she was a wreck. A total wreck.

"What did she say?" Ellie asked anxiously, as Matt returned to the *casita* a few minutes later—the longest minutes of her life.

"Well, first, you're in good health, and that goes a long way in your favor. But because you're already at risk for pre-gestational diabetes, this could help it along, so with that we've got to be very careful. And you do need to be under the care of a high-risk specialist. There's no way around that. She's suggested two different ones, but the problem is one is about four hours north of here, and the other is about four hours to the south. It would be a long, rough drive either way, but she doesn't suggest road travel until you've been checked. Which means..."

Ellie shook her head. "Which means I'm in trouble."

"Which means a helicopter. The one that hand-delivered your sample to the lab. Cruz Montoya, the owner, will charter the chopper to take you to whichever place you choose."

"You've talked to him?"

He nodded. "He's a former army medic. Good man. He said he can make the flight tomorrow, and Susie called to check availability for me. The problem is, the doctor down south in Arizona can't see you at all this week. He's not in his office. But the one up north will squeeze you in immediately because she's a friend of Susie's. They went to med school together. Cruz said it's a forty-five-minute trip by air, and Susie thinks that will be safe, especially since I'll be there with you."

"You've been busy," she said.

"Because I'm highly motivated."

"But you're in no condition to fly," Ellie stated flatly.

"And you're in no condition for me not to fly. *You can't go alone*. Besides, this will be a good chance for me to get my ribs X-rayed, just in case."

Matt's voice was so emphatic it was almost cold. But Ellie knew he was worried. It showed on his face. "In case of what? Me knowing you need those X-rays so I won't back out of this exam? And what about Lucas?"

He chuckled. "You do have a devious mind, don't you, with your ulterior motive?"

"My mother always had ulterior motives. It comes naturally."

"But you're not your mother, for starters, and you're not the kind of person who would automatically be suspicious."

"You're sure of that?"

"As sure as any man can be who sends a drink to the woman on the other side of the bar in Reno and ends up with her here in Forgeburn."

"OK, so maybe I'm stretching a little bit. But having more tests scares me, even though I know I need them."

"And I'll be right there with you, Ellie. Please, don't doubt that. Whatever happens, I'm with you these next few months, and that's a promise. And as for Lucas—

I'm going to spend the rest of the day with him, and Betty will watch him tomorrow. In the meantime, Susie said it's OK for you to go about limited activities. If you feel tired, you rest. You can ride in the truck but no ranch roads. And easy walking is fine, as long as you don't do too much of it."

"Aren't we a pair?" she said, the discouragement so thick in her voice she couldn't disguise it. "Look, Matt, I appreciate this. And I'm sorry I brought it to your doorstep. If I'd known…"

"Would you have *not* told me about the baby?" he asked, sitting down on the bed next to her.

"It never crossed my mind not to. I'm a lot of things, and I know my ambition can get in the way of what most people would consider normal, but to not tell you, to simply come up with my own solution and carry it out…" She shook her head. "That's not me. My mother maybe. My grandmother definitely. But not me."

He slipped his hand into hers. "They're tough women, but not as tough as you."

"They *are* tough, but I don't want to be like that because neither of them particularly like men. I do…obviously. And both my grandmother and mother taught me that a strong woman doesn't need a man to complete them. Whatever a woman wants, she can do on her own."

"It's true. She can. If that's what she wants."

"I know it's true, but…" She shut her eyes. "But having a man in your life doesn't have to make you weak or needy. If he's the right man."

"Which was why you came to me. You were hoping I would be the right man to raise the baby the way a baby should be raised."

"I'm the genetic by-product of my mother and grand-mother. Both cold-hearted women who didn't want children. Of course, that's what I was hoping for when I came here, hoping you'd raise our baby, and also to prove to myself that I'm not cold-hearted like they are." She ran her hand over her belly then smiled. "She's kicking."

"Or he," Matt said, as Ellie placed his hand on her belly. "Another nice strong one."

"I don't want to lose this baby, Matt. It wasn't my intention to have one, but I don't want to miscarry. This baby should have the best of everything, and while I'm not the one to give it to her, I do want her to have it."

"Which is what we're going to do."

Ellie hoped so, because the tougher this pregnancy got, the more she didn't want to go through it alone. And the only person she wanted with her was Matt. Even though his words were simple, they were encouraging. Made her feel better. Gave her the hope that everything would be fine, and she really needed that support because right now Ellie wasn't that strong woman she was pretending to be. She was merely a very scared woman, desperately trying to hang on.

"Look, since I'm allowed to ride along, why don't we go get Lucas and take him down to that little roadside café for breakfast—if Betty hasn't already fed him?"

"She hasn't. I called her after I called Susie, and Lucas was still sleeping."

"Then I'd suggest you put on some shoes…"

"Will you help me?" he asked, grinning.

"Men are so helpless," she said, grabbing a clean pair of socks, then picking up his boots.

"Is that your mother speaking?" he asked, returning her grin.

"Nope, that's me trying hard *not* to sound like my mother." She got the socks and boots on him in a matter of seconds, then headed for the *casita* door. "She's not my role model, Matt. Maybe for a while, when I was young, she was. But she's a pathetically unhappy woman, and I don't want to end up that way. I've worked very hard for many years, trying not to be my mother's daughter. And don't get me wrong. I love her like a daughter should. But she's not my friend, the way a mother should be. I talk to her occasionally, keep her updated on my life, but we live only twenty-five miles apart and we only see each other maybe twice a year. Her choice."

"And you're good with that?"

"I have to be. It's all I've ever known. So, how about we get going, although I'm not sure which one of us is more fit to drive."

"I'm fit," Matt said, following her through the house at a very slow pace.

"Yeah, right," Ellie said, holding the door open for him. "If you're even able to get yourself up into your truck."

He upped his speed, caught up to her, and slid his arm around her waist. "I'm able to do this, too," he said, as he pulled her close, then lowered his lips to hers. Ellie felt again the rush of excitement, not even thinking that she should pull away. More of this was what she wanted; what she'd wanted since Reno. That surging tide of warmth that rushed over her. The tingle that spread from her head down to her toes. And Matt's face. His beautiful face. Even though her eyes were closed, she could see it, every nuance. And wanted more. So she reached up and stroked his cheek, pulling him out of that moment, but just briefly, as he looked down at her and smiled.

"This is probably the worst thing we could be doing," he said, his voice so hushed she could barely hear him.

He was right, of course. But she didn't care. And as she twined her hand around his neck, pulling him back to her, he tilted her head up and kissed her, softly again but progressing to a shade of passion that made her cling to him like he was the only solid thing in her life. His unrelenting lips parted hers, causing her to press herself even harder to him—her, their baby, him all pressed together. And his demanding lips parted, drawing from her wild sensations she'd known only once before—with him.

It couldn't last, though. Not another second lest she be pulled even deeper into her confusion. So she backed away, the feel of him still on her lips. "What are we doing?" she asked, her voice nearly too breathless to carry her words.

"Damned if I know," he replied. His face was flushed and he was clearly aroused. "Probably something we shouldn't."

But how could something they shouldn't be doing feel so perfectly right? "I think we'd better get Lucas before we…" What? Made another mistake? Because nothing about this felt like a mistake. "…before Betty feeds him."

"Do you know how long I've wanted to do that?" he asked, not making a move to leave the house.

Ellie shook her head.

"Since the last time we did it in Reno."

"But we can't go back to Reno," she said, almost sadly. "That was another life. Two other people."

"Are you sure?" he asked, as he took her hand and led her to the truck.

No, she wasn't. And that was the problem, because the more she was around him, the less sure she was becoming about everything.

CHAPTER EIGHT

LUCAS WAS RAMBUNCTIOUS in the truck, kicking and trying to get out of his infant seat. It was like he'd been given an extra portion of energy in that single pancake he'd eaten for breakfast, and nothing Matt said or did on the drive back to the house would stop him.

It got to the point that Matt was forced to pull over and get out, then go back to the crew cab to see if anything was wrong. But there wasn't. This was simply Lucas in a good mood, laughing, playing and having fun.

"You don't suppose he understands what a pony ride is, do you?" he asked Ellie, while he pulled Lucas from the seat, rearranged him, then secured him back in. "I mean, he was right there when Betty mentioned taking him to her brother's ranch for a pony ride."

"I have no idea what someone his age understands. I have no experience with children. In fact, Lucas is the closest I've ever come to having any kind of relationship with a child, so I'm the wrong person to ask. But I will say he seems awfully bright. Maybe Betty explained what riding a pony was all about and now he's just excited to do it."

"Is that it?" Matt asked the child. Of course, Lucas

didn't answer, but Matt did notice that his eyes were shining brighter than they had before. "Are you anxious for your pony ride?"

Lucas's response was to try wiggling out of his car seat again. "Well, as soon as we take Ellie back to the house, we'll see what we can do to get you on that pony." He shut the crew cab door, climbed back in the driver's seat and exhaled a deep breath. "I'm exhausted," he said, leaning his head back against the head rest. "I didn't know so little movement could produce so much fatigue."

"But you're going to go off and be daddy. That's a good thing, Matt. Lucas needs that in his life. Someone who puts him first."

"Well, today's not going to be a very good *daddy* day."

Ellie reached over and rubbed his shoulder. "If you're with him, that's a good daddy day. That's what he depends on now."

"Says the woman who knows nothing about children."

"Says the woman who didn't have a daddy or, in essence, a mommy."

Matt looked over at her sympathetically, saw the pain flash across her eyes. Understood it. Felt it just as deeply as she did. In so many ways they were alike, and while it was always said that a person did better with an opposite, it was nice to sit here with someone who could empathize totally with Lucas and him. In ways it was like they were a family—all three of them abandoned as children, no one who had ever truly cared.

When he'd been young, Matt had wanted a family. Sometimes he'd walk up and down the streets, stop at a particularly cozy-looking house and just stand outside, wandering what it would feel like, going inside and simply being part of that family there. But in the end, he'd always returned to wherever they were staying at the moment, always knowing what to expect. *Nothing.* That's all there ever had been. It was hard growing up that way, or even the way Ellie had because nothing was nothing, no matter how rich or poor it was.

But that wasn't going to be Lucas. No matter what he had to do, Lucas was going to be the lucky one. Still, the three of them—actually, the four of them as a family—made him long for something he'd wanted all his life but hadn't had.

"Well, guess we'd better get you back to the house and get Lucas to his pony," he said, pulling back onto the road.

"If I can find a place to sit and watch, I think I'd like to go with you two," she said.

Eyes forward and hands on the steering wheel, Matt smiled. Another moment of delusion? Yes, he could handle it. Because spending time with Ellie was becoming a habit—a very nice habit. One he could get used to.

It was lovely sitting in a chair, under a tree, watching Bert Connors lead the pony around the corral while Matt held on to Lucas for dear life, even though the boy was so secured onto the pony's saddle a tornado couldn't have blown him off it.

Matt was in agony, though. It showed in his every movement. But he wasn't going to let that hamper Lucas's fun, and that was another thing she loved about him: the way he put Lucas—and even her—first. She desperately wanted Matt to raise their baby and now she couldn't even imagine anybody else doing it. Didn't want anybody else doing it. But she didn't have the heart to disturb his life any more than she already had, so that was a wish she'd have to put away.

But another plan was forming. One that was trying to poke through as hard as she was trying to push it back. Trying to ignore it. Trying to see herself in the future, doing exactly what she'd done before Reno. Except that image was beginning to blur.

"Care for a lemonade?" Francine Connors, Bert's wife, asked, holding out a glass for Ellie. "Just made it."

"I would love some," she said, bending forward slightly to take at. As she bent, though, she was hit with such a stabbing back pain that she gasped.

"You OK?" Francine asked.

Ellie leaned back in the chair, hoping the pain would go away, but it didn't. In fact, it got so bad that she doubled over and fell out of the chair to the ground. "Get Matt," she panted, scared to move, scared to breathe. This couldn't be happening. She had known it was a possibility but had never really considered that it would happen to her. Losing the baby... Tears slid down her face into the dirt, leaving small mud splotches.

"Ellie," Matt cried, dropping to his knees beside her. He took her pulse, turned her head to look at her face.

"Don't let it happen," she begged him, choking on her sobs. "Please, don't let this happen."

"We can take her inside, Doc," Francine offered. "To one of the beds."

"I don't want to move her just yet. Could you run to my truck and get my medical bag? It's in the back, in the crew cab." He glanced over at Bert, who'd taken full charge of Lucas, then pulled Ellie into his arms. "We've got to get you into a hospital," he said, taking the medical bag from Francine and immediately pulling out his stethoscope. He listened to her heart, then tried to listen for the baby's heartbeat, but since he didn't have the right equipment for that, all he could hear were normal stomach sounds.

"Francine, do you know Cruz Montoya?"

"Sure. Everybody knows him."

"Would you call him and tell him I have an emergency, that I need to get a patient to a hospital as quickly as possible. Ask him if he can fly us." He glanced down at Ellie's face again. Her eyes were shut but she was still crying softly. "Tell him stat. He'll understand." He handed Francine his phone.

While Francine made the call, Matt took Ellie's blood pressure. "How high is it?" she asked.

"Not that bad. Just the high end of normal, and that could be from stress as much as anything else. How bad are the pains?"

"Stabbing at first."

"And now?"

"Not as bad."

"Were they different from the pain you've had before?" he asked.

"I don't know," she said, glad he was there, glad for his touch, even though he was only examining her. "Why?"

"There can be a lot of different kinds of pain associated with a pregnancy. I'm just trying to figure out what's going on with you."

"You mean, it might not be…"

"I don't know, Ellie," he said, bending to kiss her

on the forehead then pulling her even closer to him. "I just don't know."

"Cruz is on his way," Francine said. "He's going to land in the back pasture so she'll have to be carried out there. But he says he has a stretcher, so not to worry."

Matt nodded. "It might be a little rough," he told Ellie, "but I'll be with you and I'll take care of you." He looked up at Francine. "Lucas…"

"Don't worry about him. I've got six grandkids. I'm used to having little ones around."

"I appreciate that," Matt said. "I lived here when I was a kid, and I don't remember the people being so… decent."

"I remember you when you were a kid," Francine said. "Didn't know you, but everybody in these parts knew how bad you had it. Felt sorry for you. I'm glad you made something of yourself."

He nodded, as the sound of a helicopter drew his attention. "Ellie, I don't want you moving, if you don't have to. Cruz and I will do all the work and the only thing you have to do is relax."

"Relax?" she asked, trying to smile. "Doctors and their unrealistic expectations." Then she shut her eyes. The pain was subsiding, but her anxiety was not. She was more scared now than she'd ever been in her life. But Matt was there, and she trusted him to get her through this. She counted on him. Needed him like she'd never needed anybody, ever.

Cruz Montoya came running with an old army stretcher in his grip. Tall, handsome, dark, with black hair, he immediately dropped to his knees next to Matt and took Ellie's pulse like it was instinctual. It was. He'd been an army medic, a fact Matt was grateful for.

"She's got a hormonal imbalance that puts her at risk for miscarriage," he explained to Cruz. "That's why I'd asked for the lift to the hospital tomorrow. But back pains are one of the symptoms that indicates something could be going wrong, and she's going through that right now. I don't want her trying to move herself."

"Easy enough," Cruz said, laying the old canvas stretcher out. "You tell me how you want us to move her and we'll get it done." He looked down at Ellie and smiled. "I'm Cruz, by the way. Tour guide to paradise and occasional air ambulance."

Matt liked him. He seemed confident, and competent. He'd only met him once before, when he'd handed over Ellie's sample, but that had been enough to know that Cruz was probably good at everything he did. At least, Matt hoped he was, because today he was going to be the one to get Ellie to the hospital.

"Let's roll her to her side, get part of the stretcher under her, then we'll lift her across it."

"Sure thing," he said, saluting Matt. "Did it just like that more times than I'd care to remember."

"You served in combat?" Ellie asked, as Matt gently rolled her to her side.

"Yep. Dispatched to Afghanistan the first time, then had a short stint close to Baghdad."

"Surprised we didn't run into each other," Matt said, as he settled Ellie down into transport position. "I was in Ramadi for a while, and had my turn in Afghanistan as well."

"I was evacuating injured de-miners—taking them to Bagram to get shipped out to a proper hospital."

Matt felt a connection to Cruz. They'd shared the same war, seen the same casualties. And both had ended up in Forgeburn. "Well, I think the evacuation we need to get on with now is Ellie."

"Which means you take her feet, I'll take her head." He smiled at Matt. "A superstition handed down to me from my dad. He did air rescue in Desert Storm. Said every time he was the one who took the head, everything turned out fine. No reason for me to break tradition."

"Hope you're right," Matt said, as they headed toward the helicopter. He hoped to God Cruz was right.

As they passed the corral, Matt waved to Lucas, who was now at the fence, watching what was going on. Bert was standing right behind him. "I'll be back in a little while," he said to the boy.

And Lucas waved back at Matt. "Bye, Daddy," he said.

"Matt," Ellie whispered.

"I know," he said, choking back tears. Damn it all. His baby was in jeopardy, so was Ellie. And Lucas was calling him Daddy. What was he going to do? What the *hell* was he going to do?

Dr. Anita Gupta smiled as she entered the exam room. "The good news is you don't have to stay. Nothing indicates you're having a miscarriage, and I'm actually leaning toward the diagnosis of severe muscle spasms. At least, for now. The bad news is, like Susie Caldwell said, you're going to have to see a maternal-fetal medicine specialist such as myself, or someone else of your choosing, every three weeks for the rest of your pregnancy, or even more if you start showing other signs of risk. Also, you must rest. I know you've heard that before, but the less you do, the better off both you and your baby will be."

"But everything's normal with the baby?" Matt asked. He was standing behind Ellie, who was still sitting on the exam table in her hospital gown, his hand on her shoulder for support. Both his own as well as hers. This wasn't the side of medicine he liked being on.

"While we didn't run a lot of specific tests, because they weren't indicated, what we saw leads us to believe everything is good. And I do know the gender of your baby, if you're interested."

Ellie twisted to look at Matt. "What do you think?"

"Sure," he said, trying to sound detached when he was anything but. Even though he'd been too nervous to check the gender when he'd looked at Ellie's ultrasound, now knowing that he could find out made the baby more of a reality than he'd expected. This was *his* baby and the idea that it would become somebody else's baby was hitting him hard.

Dr. Gupta looked to Ellie for her approval, and when she nodded, Gupta smiled even more broadly. "It's a boy."

Matt's eyes widened. "I have a son?" he asked.

"You do, Dr. McClain. Normal size, nothing to indicate problems with fetal development from what we could see. And I did have the radiologist look at it as well."

It stunned Matt, thinking in terms of his baby now having an identity. But he noticed Ellie wasn't reacting. There was no expression on her face. In fact, the look there was as cold as he'd ever seen on her. She was shutting this out. All of it. Trying not to make it personal. "Ten fingers, ten toes?" he asked, realizing he needed to be sensitive to Ellie's feelings but at the same time eager for the details for himself.

"Something like that," Dr. Gupta said. Then she addressed her next comments to Ellie. "With your back going bad, plus the stress of the trip getting you here, and I'm sure the worry over miscarrying, I want you to stick to light activity once you get back to Dr. McClain's house.

"You can drive short distances, take easy walks, go about normal chores if they don't make you too tired or cause your back to ache. There's always a fine line between allowing someone with a high-risk pregnancy to continue with daily life on a restricted basis, and sending them to bed for the duration. You're not near that line yet, and I want to keep it that way. So, please, use common sense. Like no lifting anything over five pounds, avoid using stairs as much as you can, no running.

"Oh, and no trips longer than what it takes to get you here to the hospital—by helicopter. Not driving. I don't want you on the road that long."

"What about working?" she asked.

"I hear you're a workaholic. That's got to stop. I'm going to limit you to four hours a day if you do it from home. Or Dr. McClain's home, if that's where you decide to stay. If you do go back to Reno, I'll set you up with a doctor there, but he'll probably restrict you to the same and tell you not to work from your office. I want you to have a safe, easy pregnancy, Ellie, and I want to see that son of yours born a happy, thriving baby."

Well, at least Gupta was giving Ellie some options, which was more than Matt had expected. Of course, those were daddy expectations. Not doctor expectations. Right now he wasn't sure what Ellie was feeling, but she'd be grateful that she wasn't being put on total bed rest once she got through the fright of fearing she was losing the baby. He was sure of that as she was the most determined, resilient person he'd ever met. "So we're good to go back to Forgeburn?" he asked, already texting Cruz to return.

"I don't see why not, unless Ellie doesn't feel ready. We could let her stay overnight and get rested."

"I'm fine," she said. "And I'd rather do my resting in Matt's *casita*."

Dr. Gupta held her hand out to Ellie. "It's been a pleasure meeting you, Ellie. I'll be happy to see you as your regular specialist, if that's what you choose. Or I'll make a referral to a colleague in Reno. He's very good. Either way, let me know."

"I appreciate that," Ellie said, the smile she returned to Dr. Gupta looking like it was forced.

"And you, Dr. McClain," Dr. Gupta said, extending a hand to him. "I admire the kind of practice you're attempting to run out there. It can't be easy, and I certainly wouldn't want to do what you're doing. So good luck with that. And in the future, if you run into another high-risk pregnancy, I'd certainly be glad to take the case. Or if there's any other kind of specialist you need, for *anything*, please call me. We're set up here for almost anything, and I'll be happy to connect you to the right person."

"Thank you," Matt said, deciding not to tell her his time in Forgeburn was limited. What difference would that make? Besides, saying that he was leaving was getting more and more complicated.

"I'll send the nurse in to help you dress, Ellie, then

you can check out. Call me any time if you have questions or concerns."

Ellie nodded, but didn't reply. Instead, she slipped off the exam table, stepped behind the screened dressing area without waiting for the nurse, and reappeared only moments later, dressed. As she passed by Matt on her way to the door, she didn't look at him, didn't say a word. It was like they were total strangers.

"I'm sure Lucas will be glad to see us," he said, attempting to engage her in a conversation that wasn't about her pregnancy." But she didn't engage. She merely nodded and kept on walking. He followed, not sure whether to bring up the rear or step to her side.

He opted to step to her side, and he also opted to take hold of her arm, totally expecting her to shrug him off. But she didn't. She simply let him hold on through the check-out process, then to the cab outside that would take them to the airfield. "Are you OK?" he finally asked, once they were both inside, and the miles were ticking off on the meter.

"I don't know what I am," she replied. "Today's been...rough, and I feel so isolated."

"Because of Forgeburn?" he asked.

"No. Because of me. It's like I'm walking through this in a daze. Nothing is the way it should be and there's no simple solution to fixing it. Especially now that I know I'm carrying a boy. Hearing Dr. Gupta say that makes everything too...real." Ellie sighed, and leaned her head against Matt's shoulder. "And I'm proving to myself that I'm not as strong as I've always thought I was. Maybe that's the hardest part of all."

Matt pulled her closer to him, enjoying the feel of her. "I'd gone out with the medics one day. The hospital wasn't under fire, but where I was headed was straight into the middle of it. I have this buddy, Carter Holmes. Great surgeon. A man I always counted on to have my back. He wasn't supposed to go out with me, but at the last minute he jumped on the truck, said he didn't want me out there alone.

"We were on this bad road that had already had the hell bombed out of it and Carter got motion sick, told the driver to pull over, so he could get out and, well, you can imagine what he did. Anyway, he got off the truck and I decided to go with him just to make sure he was OK. While we were out there, the truck got hit and everybody inside was killed. There was nothing we could do for any of them, it happened so fast."

He paused for a moment, took a deep breath, then continued. "Then we get shot at. I mean, we're doctors, not soldiers, and here we were in the middle of gunfire. So we looked for a place to hunker down. Found it under some rocks. Crawled in and held on.

"We were there for nearly thirty-six hours. There was fighting and gunfire all around us for two days and here we were, stuck under some rocks, no medical supplies, totally useless because we couldn't get out safely. It was a nightmare, knowing people out there might need us and we couldn't help. Listening to all that gunfire…

"For me, other than knowing I should be out there helping, it wasn't a big deal because I used to run away and hide from my dad all the time. Some of my hiding places were pretty bad. But Carter couldn't handle it. Like me, he was worried about the soldiers out there who might need a medic. It bothered both of us, but he started developing tics. Couldn't keep still. Wringing his hands. Nothing serious. Then he started mumbling and ranting, which eventually turned to screaming.

"I couldn't sedate him since I didn't have anything with me. Couldn't do anything except talk to him, and that didn't work out so well because he got to the point where he was past the ability to comprehend.

"Anyway, at the end of the first day he just got up and ran out in the open, right into the gunfire. Took a bad hit to his back, which nicked his right kidney. He was lying out there, screaming. I went after him, dragged him back to the rocks, hoping that we hadn't been spotted. But my buddy was literally dying in my arms, and there was nothing I could do except talk. Which was what I did until we were evacuated, because I was scared that if I quit talking, he'd die.

"And I felt so isolated. Nothing was right. Nothing was happening the way it should have. We had been going out for what was little more than some routine medical care, then to have all that happen... So I know where you are, Ellie, because I've been there. I was in that daze—in a situation there was no way for me to fix. And I was used to fixing things, the way you are.

"But you're wounded right now. Not like Carter was but in a sense it's the same. And the only thing I can do to help you is talk to you and take care of you the only way I know how. And listen, if you want to talk. Neither of us is in an easy place and, to be honest, all we have is each other. So don't shut me out. I'm going to get you through this the way I got Carter through it."

"He survived?" she asked.

Matt swiped at the tears that had run down his cheeks. He'd been scared in that cave, but not nearly as scared as he was now. Because this baby—it had to live. It was his child. A child he loved the way he'd never been loved. And it was Ellie, too.

"He did, but he struggles. The thing is, we all do, and we all need someone there to help us through it. Carter has a fiancée who's strong and loves him unconditionally. You and I, well, that's what it is. The two of us."

"Is this about me, Matt?" she asked. "Or only about the baby?"

"Both. But you shouldn't be alone. You need to be here, Ellie. Where I can take care of you. You need the support as much as I need to support you."

Still, he couldn't tell her that he loved her, that he might have even fallen a little in love with her in Reno, because the solution to that love wasn't easy, and it would put more stress on her than she already had. This wasn't about their jobs anymore. It was about them. With Ellie and the baby at risk, all he could think to do was support her and keep everything else away from her. Then later, after the baby was here, who knew what would happen? He sure as hell didn't.

But right now she wasn't making herself available. Even with her head on his shoulder, she was rigid. Reserved. Distant. Sighing, Matt leaned his head back against the seat, closed his eyes, then said, "I want you to stay, but the choice is up to you. If you go to Reno, so will I."

Those were the last words spoken until they reached the landing field. Then Ellie finally spoke. "I do want to stay. I think I did even before I got here."

But that still didn't solve the problem, because staying for a few months was one thing and what to do about their son was another.

* * *

Ellie was relieved, exhausted and now worried. She'd taken a big step, and it wasn't because she couldn't manage her pregnancy, even with its complication, back home. She simply didn't want to. Didn't want to be the one who didn't need anybody to lean on. She did need someone.

And that someone was Matt. He made her feel secure, made her believe that, with his help, everything would turn out all right. She'd never had that before and it was nice having someone else to go through this with her. Someone who could be strong when she wasn't. Or caring when she needed it. And she did need it, especially now that she understood what it was.

Because she loved him? Ellie was pretty sure she did. It hadn't taken long to fall, but she had. And, of course, it was an almost impossible situation. She had some time to figure it out, though, now that she was going to stay. Would that time do her any good? She didn't know. In fact, she didn't know his true feelings for her. Matt showed affection, said the right words, did the right things, but was that more out of his sense of duty, or was it genuine? Because if it was genuine...

"What about going back to active duty?" she asked him a few minutes later as she lowered herself onto the bed in the *casita*. "Have you worked that out?"

"That's not for you to worry about. I'm in good standing with the army, so I'm not going to have any problems making some changes."

"But I don't want to be the one to hold you back from your career." She lifted her feet onto the bed and dropped back into the pillows.

"You're not," Matt said, as he sat down on the edge

of the bed next to her, then took her hand in his and stroked it gently. "And the only thing you have to worry about is taking care of yourself."

"But I worry about you, too, Matt. I put you on a detour you didn't expect. When the army told me you'd gone home, I thought… If I'd known you were still active in the military, I would have handled everything differently, without asking you to raise the baby. Being practical, the way I usually have been until now, I would have seen that you couldn't."

"Our son, Ellie. The baby is *our son*."

She was aware of that, but saying it out loud nearly broke her heart because the moment she'd heard it was a boy, she'd given him a name. Matthew. After his father. And she'd pictured little Matthew growing up with Lucas as brothers. The four of them together, as a family. "I know we need to talk about that, but I'm so tired. Maybe tomorrow?"

"Works for me, since I've got to get Lucas. I need some time with him. Especially since…" He swallowed hard.

"Since he called you Daddy?"

Matt shook his head. "Don't know what to do about that."

"Maybe you don't do anything and let it work itself out on its own." And again the image of a family of four popped into her mind.

"Well, however it works out, Lucas needs to be home. So…" He leaned over and brushed a light kiss to her forehead. But she snaked her arm around his neck and pulled him to her mouth.

She wanted that kiss. It wasn't right. It wouldn't lead to anything. But it was the only thing on her mind and she was, if nothing else, a decisive person. This was what she wanted. The kiss. To see his reaction. To go to sleep with Matt on her mind, and not all her worries.

But he pulled away before they'd really started. "That part of us is easy," he said. "Too easy. Which is why we shouldn't..." He shook his head and backed away. "Look, I'll be back in a while. Is there anything you need before I go?"

There was. But unlike the easy part of them, it was hard. Too hard.

"It should be a short day," Matt told Ellie the next morning as he came down for breakfast. She was already sitting at the kitchen table, helping Lucas eat his breakfast. Or more like playing with him as he did. "No one on a ranch, and only a handful of scheduled appointments. If any tourists come in, or I get an emergency call, that could delay me, but as it is right now I should be home shortly after lunchtime."

It was difficult facing her, after rejecting her last night. But he'd done what he'd had to do because both of them were playing volleyball with their emotions, and it wasn't getting them anywhere. He was especially worried about Ellie. She didn't need that kind of tension, which meant he was the one who would have to make sure things were slow and easy with them. For her good and, in a way, his own good as well.

"And you're taking Lucas with you?'

Matt chuckled, and patted Lucas on the head. "Us men need some bonding time. And Betty went to see her sister, so..."

"I could watch him."

"Or you could rest. Besides, he's too heavy for you to pick up, so for now this hombre is with me."

"You're probably right but, still, if you get in a bind, we could work something out."

"I appreciate that," he said. "But it's going to be tough enough on him when he leaves, being bonded to me. I don't want him to have to go through the same thing with you as well." Even as he said the words, Matt hated them. But Ellie offered no stability on which to pin any hopes, dreams or expectations. And he couldn't allow that to enter Lucas's life. So, for now, he had to take care that he would be the only one to break the little boy's heart. Which broke his own heart.

"Anyway…" He scooped Lucas into his arms and headed for the front door, glad the pain from his injury had substantially subsided. "If you're up to it when we get through, I'll take you to lunch at the new resort a few miles from here. I want to get acquainted with the manager since I'll be on call for them. If you want to go."

"I might," she said, her voice unusually emotionless. "Call me before you make the drive back, so you won't make a wasted trip if I'm not up to it."

He didn't want to leave it like that, but he had to. Right now, he had everybody's best interests to juggle, and the most he could do was just separate them and see what happened. And pray something better *would* happen.

Opening her laptop and fighting back tears at the same time, Ellie wanted to attribute the tears to hormones, but she couldn't. Matt had hurt her, not letting her watch Lucas. She understood why, but that didn't make her pain any less. And that after his rejection the night before, which she also understood. Another thing she understood was that because of both rejections he was, most likely, planning on getting out from under all of it. Of course, that's what he'd said from the beginning.

Still, as her feelings about their baby had been changing, Ellie had hoped his were changing as well. But they weren't. She'd been hopeful, though. Not fully confident but hopeful. Yet here she was, stuck with new feelings and a different vision than she'd ever planned for herself. She wanted to keep her baby—a thought that had been running in and out of her mind since she'd learned she was pregnant, but wasn't brave enough to admit.

She wanted to raise him, see him grow up to be just like his father. And she would. She wasn't her mother. She *could* give her baby everything he needed and still do her job. It would be tough, doing it alone. But after she'd felt that first kick, and Matt had felt it, she'd known what she would do, even if her stubborn self wasn't quite ready to admit it yet.

Ellie loved this child with all her heart. Which was why she'd never considered abortion, and why she was so very careful in her choices now that she was high-risk. She thought Matt did, too. Or maybe he didn't. Maybe that was simply what she wanted to see in him when he couldn't see it in himself.

Whatever the case, no one was going to adopt this baby. In fact, she had a mind to adopt one more. Maybe they wouldn't be a family of four, but a family of three would be good. Her, baby Matthew and Lucas. Then Matt could have his life back without worries.

"Guess what, Matthew?" she said as she laid her hand across her belly. "We're going to be together, forever, just the three of us." Words that should have cheered her but somehow even made her sadder. Because she still pictured Matt there. He was in her mental image of a perfect family, and also in her heart. But he wasn't going to be in her real family, and that hurt her more than anything ever had.

CHAPTER NINE

DAMN, HE HATED THIS. Not the job. Not even Forgeburn so much anymore. Being away from it for so long had changed Matt's perspective, and while he still didn't have that coming-home feeling, he was remembering how much he'd liked the area.

What he hated, though, was how he was going back and forth. He wanted to raise his son, and Lucas, yet he wasn't sure he was good enough. There was always that deep-seated fear of becoming his father in the back of his mind. And while it was never very prominent, he saw how Ellie struggled with the same thing, trying not to be her mother.

Neither one of them had been raised by good parents, and while he thought that should have forged a strong bond between them, he didn't feel that it had. The struggle was real, and ongoing. And there were now two babies in the balance.

"OK, Mr. Albright, let's have a listen to your chest." He placed a stethoscope on the elderly man's chest and heard bilateral wheezing, which was what he'd expected to hear from a three-pack-a-day smoker. "It's still emphysema," he said. "And like the last doctor said, you need to give up smoking."

"I need a tank of oxygen like you see all them people in the city toting around."

"Can't prescribe you oxygen while you're still smoking. Oxygen supports combustion, and if you decide to smoke while you're wearing your cannula, you could set yourself on fire. Give up the cigarettes and you'll get your oxygen."

It was a terrible solution, but the man had palsied hands, and that added to the recipe for disaster. If he missed his aim when going to light his cigarette, and he was wearing his oxygen cannula, well—Matt didn't even want to think about that. He'd treated too many burns on the battlefield. They were hideous and, in Mr. Albright's feeble condition, he wouldn't survive them.

"Take your aerosol treatments the way you've always done, and cut back the smokes. If you can't do that, and your breathing gets worse, we may have to talk about sending you to a rehab facility where they won't allow you to smoke, and they'll give you the oxygen you'll need."

"Not going there, Doc. You can't force me. And those aerosol treatments—haven't done one of them in months. They're worthless." He drew in a deep breath, wheezed out a cough, then scooted to the edge of the exam table. "As worthless as you are."

Matt didn't respond. Instead, he opened the exam-room door and watched Mr. Albright make his way out of the clinic. Some people simply wouldn't be helped, he thought as he returned to his cubby-hole office to make his notes.

James Albright, advanced emphysema. Heavy smoker—three packs per day. Bilateral sonorous wheezing. Clubbed fingers. Slight cyanosis both fingernails and lips. At risk: cardiac complications, pneumothorax, bullae. Possible signs of mental confusion. Refuses aerosol treatments, refuses to quit smoking. Doctor refuses oxygen due to feebleness and high burn risk. Recommendation: long-term care facility. Patient refuses to go.

"Stubborn old coot," Matt said to himself as he closed the Albright file then took a peek in at Lucas, who was playing a toddler video game. "I'll be right back," he told the boy. "Just going next door to check supplies before we leave." Which took all of five minutes.

"It's not right," James Albright shouted from Matt's office as he emerged from the supply room several minutes later.

He'd come back, and Matt was *so* not in the mood to argue with him. "What's not right?" Matt asked him as he entered the office, only to find that Albright had made himself at home and was sitting behind his desk, not in front of it as patients were supposed to do. "And why is the door open?" he choked, referring to the Dutch door.

"To let the kiddie in there out. He was calling for Daddy, so I let him out to go find his daddy."

Matt's heart skipped a beat. "Did you see where he went?"

"Why would I care? He's not my kid."

"Lucas," Matt called, running out of his office and starting his search in the exam room. Then the public toilet. Then the waiting area. But there was no sign of him. "Lucas," he called over and over, rechecking the same areas, as Mr. Albright stood and watched. "Are you sure you didn't see where he went?" Matt cried desperately one last time.

But all Albright did was shrug.

"When did you come back in?" he asked, trying to control his temper.

"Turned around as soon as I got outside and came right back to tell you you're worthless."

Which meant Lucas had been gone at least five minutes or more. But where was he? Was there someplace to hide in the clinic he didn't know about? Someplace only a toddler could fit? Had he looked under the desk in the waiting room? Or in the cabinets in the exam room? That's where he had to be. One of those places. Matt chose the waiting room to begin another search, and this time he saw it.

The clinic door was standing wide open. Which meant— Dear God! He'd gone outside. That could be a good thing, though, Matt said to himself as he ran out the door. A child his size couldn't have gone far in that short amount of time. So, with a little hope returning, Matt ran to the parking lot, shouted Lucas's name, then turned in one direction after another, expecting to see him. But he didn't. So he ran to the other side of the building and did the same. Then to the road. And back to the clinic. By now, his panic had become so overwhelming he was shaking. Sweating. Nauseous.

"Lucas," he kept calling as Albright got into his truck and pulled out of the parking lot, not even offering to help.

And the clock ticked off another five minutes, which meant Lucas had been gone for ten.

Where could a toddler go in ten minutes? And where

should he look? If he went in one direction but Lucas was wandering off in the opposite direction… Standing in the middle of the parking lot, Matt turned around in a circle one last time, looking everywhere. But saw nothing. He needed help. But he also needed to get out there and look. Maybe Ellie—she could call people.

"Ellie," he choked into the phone when she picked up. "Lucas is missing. I need help."

"When? How?"

"Sometime in the last ten minutes. One of my patients let him out of the playroom, and he wandered out the door."

"You've checked everywhere in the clinic?" she asked.

"Yes. He's not there. I've got to start searching away from the clinic. With all the rocks and canyons… What I need you to do is call people and ask for help. I need people out here, searching with me. Start with Francine and Bert. Lucas might be trying to get there for another pony ride. Maybe call some of the hotels and businesses and ask them to keep an eye out as well."

"Is there anything else I can do?" she asked Matt.

He wished there was. But putting her under even more stress scared him. "No. Just take care of yourself. And, Ellie, I'm sorry about—well, a lot of things." That was all he said before he clicked off and headed toward the dry river bed that was in view of the clinic. It was close, and it was as good a place to start searching as any. "Lucas," he called out in that direction. "Just stay where you are, buddy. I'm coming to get you."

He prayed those weren't empty words.

Everyone was called, search parties were being organized to meet at the clinic, Cruz was taking to the air, and she was about ready to jump out of her skin. Ellie paced the house, end to end, for about five minutes, then headed to her car. Maybe she couldn't get involved in the vigorous search, but she had to do something, and driving within reason was approved.

She looked at the clock on her phone and, by all estimations, Lucas had been missing for nearly an hour now. She hadn't heard back from Matt, so there was no optimism there. And among the people gathering for the search there were no trained search and rescue experts—just concerned residents. A group of rangers were coming in, but not for another hour. So there wasn't as much optimism as she'd hoped for there either.

Overhead, the sound of a helicopter went from soft to loud, and she looked up to see Cruz heading east, which would take him away from the clinic. Being so high, would he even be able to see someone as tiny as Lucas?

With a sigh and a prayer, Ellie climbed into her car and headed straight to the clinic to see what was being organized. Maybe she wouldn't be much help, but she'd feel better just being where the activity was. And maybe she'd catch sight of Matt somewhere along the way. She really needed to see him, to reassure him, to have him reassure her.

Ellie drove slowly along the way, looking up and down both sides of the road. Realistically, Lucas couldn't have come this far in only an hour. She was three miles from the clinic, the only one on the road—probably because everybody else knew what she'd only just figured out. Still, she looked. Saw cactus in bloom, lots of open space, a few cattle grazing here and there, a rundown cowboy trailer.

On a whim, she took the ranch road up to the trailer,

glad it wasn't as bumpy as some, and stopped near the front door. She looked around, saw no sign that anybody was there, but she knocked anyway since it was open. No answer, though.

She decided to take one look around the trailer before she got back on the road, and halfway to the rear she ran into an old man who was tinkering with something in his shed. His rusty truck was parked off to the side, its door part open, its windshield so dirty she wondered how anybody could see out of it to drive. And his yard—it was so cluttered she had to watch every step lest she trip over something and fall.

"There's a little boy gone missing," she said. "Search parties are out looking. You wouldn't have happened to see him, would you?"

The man spun around, his face fixed in a dark glare, and stared at her for a moment. "What I see is a trespasser," he said.

"I'm looking for a lost child," she said emphatically. "Since you live near the place where he went missing…"

"Don't give a damn about lost kids," he hissed. "If the parents aren't smart enough to look out for them in these parts, that's their fault. Not mine. I don't want no part of it. So get off my property. Go look for your kid somewhere else." He turned his back to her and continued what he'd been doing, giving Ellie no choice but to leave. Stopping here had been a long shot anyway, since Lucas simply couldn't have come this far. She wouldn't have felt right if she hadn't stopped, though.

And what a rude man. He was the first rude person she'd made contact with in Forgeburn, but maybe he was just bitter about being past his cowboy days because he clearly was well past them. She sympathized with him a little, wondering how she'd feel if time and age had robbed her of who she was. And that man had been a cowboy. His saddle was resting on a sawhorse, exposed to the weather, probably not used in a long, long time. That's not the way she wanted to end up and now, more than ever, she knew she was on the right course, keeping her baby, adopting Lucas. But Lucas—dear God, she was so scared.

Back on the road, Ellie finally came to the clinic, where several people were still trying to figure out which way to go. She got out of the car, talked to a few of them, and nothing anybody said made her feel easier. The people here were well intentioned, but their searches were random. Even Ellie, who'd had no experience at this, could see that. "Has Matt been back to the clinic?" she asked Francine, who was setting out drinks for those involved. "I've tried raising him on the phone, but nothing goes through."

"Haven't seen or heard from him. Someone said he started at the dry creek bed over there..." Francine pointed to it. "But who knows which direction he went?"

"And he's by himself?" Ellie asked. Matt was still in no condition to do this. Granted, his injuries weren't serious, as confirmed by the X-rays he'd had while she'd been in the hospital, but they were still painful enough that she feared they might compromise him in some way. He was a soldier, though. Smart. Trained in rescue. He'd survived the battlefield, and keeping his friend alive while being shot at. That did give her hope, but she couldn't help worrying, nonetheless.

She loved that man. Loved that little boy. They'd changed her life in so many ways in such a short time, it had to mean she'd been ready to change and only waiting for the right one or, in the case, ones to do it. Matt and Lucas were the ones. And her baby. There was no doubt in her heart that they were the only ones. And now one of them was in such danger...

"Look, I'm restricted because of pregnancy complications, but I'm going to drive a little way out and see what I can see from the road. If Matt comes back, tell him I'm here but I'm taking care of myself. Will you do that for me, Francine?"

Francine took hold of Ellie's hand and squeezed it. "Of course I will, dear. But, please, watch out for yourself. The way Matt's eyes light up when he talks about you—he wouldn't want you taking chances. Not with yourself, not with his baby."

Ellie was surprised he'd told anyone about the baby. "He told you it was his?"

Francine shook her head. "No. But that day at the ranch when you keeled over—there was no doubting it. Especially with the way he was looking at you, and the way you were looking at him. Pure love I was seeing in both of you."

The way he'd looked at her—pure love. Those were the words that ran through her mind as she climbed into her car and headed down the road. Could Matt... did he actually love her? It was too much to hope for, too much to think about right now. Yet...

Matt glanced at his watch—yes, he was one of those who still relied on his watch and not his phone for the time. Lucas had been missing for an hour and a half, and he simply could not have come this far. He'd seen some of the people out looking, seen Cruz pass overhead a few times, but he was so damn discouraged he didn't know what to do.

Somebody should have found Lucas by now. A toddler on the loose couldn't have gotten that far, and because no one had spotted him that could mean— Matt didn't even want to think about all the rocks and canyons out here. Damn, he didn't want to think about them, but that's all that was on his mind—Lucas falling off a rock, or into a canyon, lying there hurt in a place where no one would ever find him.

Bye, Daddy...

Those words were on his mind. He *was* Daddy, wasn't he? To Lucas, to his own baby. Sure, maybe he'd tried to ignore that fact, or hide behind the complications, but he wasn't going to do that anymore. Lucas was in danger. Ellie was struggling to keep their baby alive and healthy. And here he was, always looking for a way out.

"Stupid," he said, as he trudged toward the road that would take him back to the clinic. There, he'd regroup and start over. And call Ellie. He needed to talk to her. Needed to hear her tell him that they'd find Lucas, that everything would be OK. Because on his own, he sure as hell didn't believe that.

When he got to the road, the only thing he could see was a distant car, heading very slowly in his direction. Someone out looking, he guessed, glad for the support from Forgeburn that he'd never had as a kid. It was a different community now. Or maybe he was different. Whatever the case, they'd come together for him and there were no words to describe his appreciation. So, could he stay here? Keep the practice, his son *and* Lucas, and stay?

That was the question he was contemplating when the car finally came close enough to identify. Ellie! Damn, she shouldn't be doing this, yet he was so glad to see her. "Ellie," he called running toward the car as it came to stop in a cloud of dust.

She was out of the car and in his arms in a flash. "Everybody's looking, Matt. More and more people are showing up to help."

"Are you OK?" he asked, unwilling to let her out of his arms.

"I'm fine."

"You know you shouldn't be out here."

"Where else could I be?" she asked. "I couldn't just sit at home and wait. That's not me."

"I know it's not you," Matt said tenderly, finally loosening his hold on her. "It's not going well. He couldn't have gone that far, and…" His words choked off. He couldn't say them aloud.

"We're going to find him, Matt. He's been out for a while. I'll bet he's probably crawled off into a shady spot to nap. It *is* his naptime, you know."

He tried to manage a smile, but it simply wasn't in him. "We, um—when we get Lucas back home, and we're all rested, you and I need to have a talk. There are some things—stupid things I've been holding on to, and I can't go on like this."

"Me, too," she said, brushing his cheek with her hand. "But right now how about I give you a ride back to the clinic? Francine's got some lemonade and other drinks going. You get yourself rehydrated, and maybe by then…"

"Maybe by then," he said, as he climbed into her car.

Maybe by then, but probably not, because there was no optimism left in him. None at all.

"Are you sure you're up to it?" she asked Matt, as he prepared to go back out and join the thirty-five other people who were now engaged in the search. "Maybe you should rest a little while longer."

"Can't," he said, swigging on his third glass of iced water. "If Lucas is out there, that's where I've got to be."

"First, tell me exactly what happened. Tell me about the patient who let him out."

"He's a crotchety old guy. Has advanced emphysema and it's probably muddling his mind like it can do sometimes. He said he turned Lucas loose to find his daddy."

"OK, so maybe the guy has a problem. But did he leave the front door open as well?"

"Probably, since he'd just come through it."

Ellie shook her head. "Well, there's nothing we can do about that, but…" The rest of her words were drowned out by Cruz, in his helicopter, who circled once then started to land just off the end of the parking lot. Within a matter of a couple of minutes he was there with them.

"I'm a pretty good spotter. That was half the battle when I was rescuing in the army. But some of this area is so rugged I can't see as well as I'd like and, to be honest, I'm not as fast as I should be because of that. Didn't get as much area covered as I'd intended. Matt, would you want to come up with me for a while, so I can focus on the flying while you focus on the looking? I've been over every place I think he could have gone in the time he's been out there, given his age, but there are a few…"

he swallowed hard "…less obvious places I want to get down into, and I can't do that alone."

Matt nodded. He understood. So did Ellie, as she fought to control tears that wanted to escape. The canyons, the rocks… She couldn't bear to think that Lucas might be— She reached over and squeezed Matt's arm. But neither of them spoke. She stepped forward and kissed him, though, before he went off with Cruz. And as the helicopter lifted into the sky, she went to Lucas's playroom in the clinic, sat down on the floor, and cried harder than she'd ever cried in her life.

Twenty minutes later, still racked with dry sobs, Ellie finally got up, then ran her fingers over the lock on the bottom half of the Dutch door. Matt was so proud of this room. A perfect solution for Lucas when he was at the clinic. She looked at the lock, hating the man who'd opened the door, even though there was a possibility that he had problems. But she couldn't help herself. Brain complications or not, he'd left two doors open, and now Lucas might be dead because of that. The unthinkable thought now in her mind, she wanted to cry again, but she needed to get back out there and do her little part, even though she was so limited, sticking only to the paved roads.

Sighing, and not caring that her face was still red and bloated, Ellie headed for her car, climbed in, then wondered which way to go. She'd covered everything she could near the clinic, but not the terrain where Lucas might have encountered the rocks and canyons. And Matt and Cruz were now flying over those. Plus, there were so many people going in so many directions…

Maybe she should go back the way she'd come. Maybe somehow Lucas was trying to get home. Although she doubted that since he was so young. But Ellie was desperate. She needed to be out there, looking. So, she headed back down the road toward home, passed the same cacti she'd passed a little while ago. Passed by the crotchety old cowboy's trailer… She got to about a hundred yards away, then jammed on the brakes. Crotchety? No. There was no connection. Could there be?

She looked up, saw Cruz's helicopter in the distance, dipping into a canyon, and she held her breath until it came back out. Looked back at the trailer, then put her car into reverse. OK, so he wouldn't be happy to see her again. But she had to go back. Ask one more time. Because—two crotchety old guys in Forgeburn? Sure, it could happen. The people she'd met here were nice, but that didn't necessarily mean everyone was nice. And the odds that Forgeburn had two old crotchety guys, or maybe even more, were high. She had to look again, though. One more try. Something was pulling her to do it. Something she'd never felt before. Something—maternal?

Whatever it was, Ellie walked straight to the back of the trailer, right past the sawhorse with the saddle, right past the rusty old truck, right up to the old cowboy, who was sitting in a yard chair now, his back to her. Huffing and puffing like he couldn't get his breath. Emphysema? Like Matt's patient. "Where is he?" she shouted at the man.

"Who?" he asked, not even bothering to turn to see who it was.

"The boy who's missing. Where is he?" She looked up as Cruz passed overhead, and jumped up and down, waving, hoping Matt would see her. But he didn't. The yard was too full of junk, she was too concealed. And the helicopter just kept going. "The boy you let out of his playroom at the clinic. Where is he?" She stepped directly in front of the man and repeated herself. "Where is he?"

"Don't know what you're talking about," he said. "Now get off my property, and I'm not telling you again."

"You took him," she hissed, and bent over to get closer to him. "You took him, and you'd better tell me…"

Her back caught, and she stood up. The pain was sudden and overwhelming, and she prayed it was only a back spasm, as Dr. Gupta had told her the other incident had been. Drawing in a deep breath, she let it out slowly, and as she did so she saw something through the dirty window of the old truck. It was moving. Then suddenly it was gone. She blinked, then walked deliberately toward the truck as she couldn't run. The pain was increasing with every moment. She had to look, though. Had to know…

Then it hit her. The truck's door was open. She'd noticed that before. Open the way he'd left the playroom door open and the clinic's door. Even his own front door. An indication of his dementia, possibly. She wanted to hurry her pace, wanted Cruz to fly back over and spot her—but she was on her own now. This was up to her. "Lucas," she called. "Can you hear me?"

There was no response as she finally made it to the front of the truck. Then the side, and the open door. Where she found Lucas, sitting in the driver's seat, his hands on the steering wheel, like he was pretending to drive. "Lucas," she said, as the tears ran down her face. "I'm so glad to see you."

"Daddy?" he asked, looking over at her.

"I'll take you to him," she said, climbing into the truck and taking the boy into her arms. "He's been looking for you, and he'll be very happy to see you."

Lucas looked up at her, ever so innocently, then snuggled into her arms. And there they sat for the next several minutes as her back pains grew worse. But she had Lucas, and that's all that mattered.

"I'm right behind you," Cruz called, making sure his helicopter was secure before he followed Matt back to that old cowboy trailer.

Matt was already so far ahead, though, that he didn't hear. All he knew was that he'd seen Ellie down there, seen her signal. And the few minutes that had ensued before Cruz could set down had been the longest of his life. What was she doing there? Did she have Lucas? Was she in trouble? Too many thoughts tossed around in his brain as he pounded the dirt, running harder and faster than he ever had in his life, despite his injuries.

Finally, when he got there, he saw James Albright. Sitting in a chair. Coughing and wheezing. But no Ellie, and there was no way that Albright, in his condition, could have done anything to her. He looked toward the front of the trailer, saw her car, which meant—

"Ellie?" he called.

"Over here," came the response from an old truck sitting amongst all the junk.

Immediately, he was there, looking in the driver's side window. Then climbing in and pulling both Ellie and Lucas into his arms. "Are you OK?" he asked her.

"No," she said. "I'm not."

* * *

Matt studied the IV drip in Ellie's arm, then looked down at her. She was stable, the baby was fine. But this was the rest of her pregnancy. In bed. Resting. No work. No rescue operations. He took her hand and kissed it as he sat down on the edge of her bed.

"How's Lucas?" she asked him.

"Fine. No signs of trauma. I talked to the sheriff in the area who was assigned to investigate, and he thinks Lucas simply walked out of the clinic and got into Albright's truck, maybe thinking it was mine. Since Albright has a habit of leaving doors open, his truck door might have been open, making it easy for Lucas to climb in. There's a strong possibility that Albright didn't even know Lucas was there."

"Where is Lucas now?" she asked.

"On the back of a pony. A lot of people volunteered to watch him for a couple of days while I'm here with you."

"You don't have to stay, Matt. Lucas needs you now."

"So do you." He laid his hand on her belly. "And, so does our son."

"We need to talk about that," Ellie said. "Dr. Gupta's fairly optimistic that I can go to term, or near term. And she's approved the helicopter rides back and forth, since she'll be seeing me pretty much every other week now.

"But do you really want me to stay with you, because this isn't going to be easy. I think all I'm going to be allowed to do is chew and swallow, which means the burden of my care will be, well…up to you. And while I know you've promised to stay, is that really what you want to do? Because I've changed my mind about some things that will allow you to get back the life you want."

"Such as?" Matt asked, his face growing a little clouded with concern.

"I'm going to keep the baby. Raise him the way he needs to be raised. You don't have to be involved in that, since it's my decision and not yours. And the second thing—I talked to your social worker about Lucas a little while ago. I'm going to adopt him. I love him like he's mine, and I can't see him going to someone else. I'm pretty sure you'll approve me, because it's a good thing that the boys will be raised together."

"Want me to tell you about my plan?" Matt asked. "Because I have one, too."

Ellie shut her eyes and drew in a deep breath. "Is it going to break my heart?" she asked. "Because I really want the boys and me to be a family."

"Well, your plan is a good one, but it will be a perfect one if I'm included in it."

She opened her eyes, clearly startled. "What do you mean?" she asked cautiously.

"It starts with this—will you marry me, Ellie?"

"Because of the baby?"

"Because of you. You are the most engaging, hard-driven, optimistic woman I've ever known. I think I fell a little in love with you in Reno, and I've fallen the rest of the way in love with you here, in Forgeburn. Now I love you even more for wanting to adopt Lucas, but I think I've known all along I wouldn't give him up. I just chose to ignore the obvious because of, well, so many things. My past mostly. It's hard to move forward when you're so stuck in the past. Hard moving forward if you think you're going to be rejected, too."

"You thought I'd reject you?"

"Your plan was always about going back to Reno."

"Because your plan was always about going back to the army. What was I supposed to do?"

"Actually, we both did the same thing. We hid from our feelings, partly because neither of us wanted to be rejected the way we were when we were kids. And partly because it's scary changing your life so drastically when you've found it to be the safe haven you've never had before. I love you, Ellie Landers. And if part of that means moving to Reno with you, I'll do it."

"But I don't want to go back to Reno," Ellie said. "Part of my plan—the part I never thought would happen—was staying here, raising our boys together. But you were always so dead set on getting back to being an army surgeon, I thought I couldn't compete with that."

"You started competing with that the first time I laid eyes on you, only I was too stupid to see it. And while I haven't been consciously aware of how I was dealing with my feelings, getting rid of Lucas, not raising our baby, not getting involved with you the way I wanted to—that's all part of the way I cope. Maybe leaving Janice behind was, too. I don't know.

"But that's not who I want to be. That was the kid who lived in the dump. But I'm not that kid anymore. The one who always ran away. I'm the man who wants to be your husband, and father to our boys. The man who wants to stay."

"I would never hurt you, Matt. And leaving you—no. I didn't want to do that. Not after I saw who you were. But my first reaction was how am I going to live the life I've been *trained* to live with a child? I took the easy way out. Dumped the decisions about what to do on you.

"But then…there was you. A completely different matter. Plus Lucas. A ready-made family for the woman who was so career-oriented she couldn't see anything else around her. I was hiding behind my career like you were hiding behind yours. Always telling myself I wanted, even needed bigger and better. But you, Lucas and our baby—that's what I need. All I need. That's my bigger and better, and I only came to realize that after I realized I wasn't my mother. My bigger and better isn't hers, and hers isn't mine."

She smiled. "And mine's so much better than hers will ever be. So, yes, I want to marry you. More than that, I need to marry you, and not because I'm pregnant but because we are a family—the four of us. We need to be together."

"Then will it be Reno or Forgeburn?" he asked, reaching over to brush a tear from her cheek. "Or someplace else, where we can start over?"

"We've already started over right here, in Forgeburn. This is where I want to stay. I'll keep my company. Just move the facilities here, if that's what you want. I like it here. Like the people here. And despite your bad memories, which I want to help you deal with, this is the place I want to raise our boys. The people are good. I love the desert.

"And when you give up your practice here to go back into the army, we can find another house or maybe buy this one—that is, if you want to stay here. If you don't, well, anywhere. I'll even go with you overseas when I'm allowed. I know some military families get to go. And the boys and I—we'll follow you when we can. And wait for you to come home when we can't."

"No following," he said. "I want my family to have stability. Besides, I'm only going to be gone a few days every month, working at a veterans' hospital. As a surgeon. Then the rest of the time I'll be here, as a GP.

"How?"

"Remember when I told you the army had options. My option was to vacate my contract and transition into the reserves to serve the rest of my active duty. I'll be in for a longer period of time but working only a few days at a time. So I've already started the process of buying the practice and the house from Doc Granger. Oh, and so you'll know, I wouldn't have let our baby be put up for adoption either. I fell in love with him the moment I knew you were carrying him. Just didn't want to admit it, like everything else I didn't want to admit."

"That first day when Lucas called you Daddy..."

"That's when I knew," he admitted. "Knew I was being stupid in so many ways. Knew what I wanted. Knew that it scared me to death. Knew that we were meant to be a family." He bent over and kissed her lightly on the forehead. "It won't be an easy life. I can't promise you much except my love."

"And a life I never thought I could have. That's what I've wanted, Matt. Like you, I didn't want to admit it because changing a life is so difficult, and I've had to do it so many times, trying to find out who I really am. Who I am, though, isn't so complicated after all. I'm the woman who wants to be part of her family. Wife, mother and, yes, career woman. With you, Lucas, Matthew—"

"Matthew?" he interrupted.

"That's what I've named him. I don't know your middle name but I want him to have that, too."

"No, you don't," he said, putting on a fake cringe.

"What is it?" she asked him.

"First, tell me your name. I don't have a clue what it is."

"It's Eleanor Landers, NMI."

"What's NMI?"

"No middle name. My mother believed middle names were useless, and being the practical woman she is she didn't give me one. And before you ask, she only named me Eleanor because it was convenient. It was the name of the nurse who helped deliver me. Apparently, my mother hadn't had time to choose my name, so when they asked her, she looked at the nurse's nametag and that's the name I got."

"Be glad it wasn't Brunhilde," he said, chuckling.

"Actually, I got lucky. I like my name. But, apparently you don't like your middle name?"

He shook his head.

"No secrets in this relationship, Matt. So tell me."

"Strandrew," he admitted.

"Strandrew? I've never heard of that." She lifted her hand to her mouth to cover a giggle. "Matthew *Strandrew* McClain."

"What can I say? I think my dad was drunk when he filled out the paperwork. I'm pretty sure it was supposed to be Andrew. At least, that's what I've always told myself." Her laugh was infectious, and he joined in.

"Matthew *Andrew*," she finally said. "I could get used to that. But you're right. *Not* Strandrew." She wrinkled her nose, just saying the name again.

"So, now that we've named our son, and you've accepted my marriage proposal, what's next?"

"Call the hospital chaplain, then happily-ever-after?"

"Definitely happily-ever-after," he said, stretching out on the hospital bed next to her when she scooted over and patted the spot where she wanted him. "And would that begin with a kiss?"

"Or maybe a kick to the belly," she said, placing his hand on her belly.

"And a kiss," he said, leaning over but kissing her belly, as their son was still kicking inside her. "I think he knows he's the one who brought us back together, where we belong," Matt said when baby Matthew finally calmed down.

"I think you're right," Ellie said, scooting over a little more to cuddle in with Matt. "Now, how about a kiss for the mommy?"

* * * * *

COMING SOON!

We really hope you enjoyed reading this book. If you're looking for more romance, be sure to head to the shops when new books are available on

Thursday
23rd August

MILLS & BOON

Coming next month

THE NURSE'S PREGNANCY MIRACLE
Ann McIntosh

Nychelle tried with all her might to say they shouldn't go any further, but couldn't get the words out. Knowing she needed to tell him the rest of her story battled with the desire making her head swim and her body tingle and thrum with desire.

'Tell me you don't want me,' he said again, and she knew she couldn't. To do so would be to lie.

'I can't. You know I can't. But...'

He didn't wait to hear the rest, just took her mouth in a kiss that made what she'd planned to say fly right out of her brain.

Desire flared, hotter than the Florida sun, and Nychelle surrendered to it, unable and unwilling to risk missing this chance to know David intimately, even if it were just this once. Was it right? Wrong? She couldn't decide — didn't want to try to.

There were so many more things she should explain to him, but she knew she wouldn't. Telling him about the baby when she knew he didn't want a family would destroy whatever it was growing between them. It was craven, perhaps even despicable not to be honest with him, and she hated herself for being underhand, but her mind, heart and body were at war, and she'd already accepted which would win.

She'd deal with the fallout, whatever it might be, tomorrow. Today—this evening—she was going to have what she wanted, live the way she wanted. Enjoy David for this one time. There would only be regrets if she didn't.

His lips were still on hers, demanding, delicious. She'd relived the kisses they'd shared over and over in her mind, but now she realized memory was only a faded facsimile of reality. The touch and taste and scent of him encompassed her, overtaking her system on every level.

Her desperate hands found their way beneath his shirt, and his groan of pleasure was as heartfelt as her joy at the first sensation of his bare skin beneath her palms. His hands, in turn, explored her yearning flesh, stroking her face, then her neck. When they brushed along her shoulders, easing the straps of her sundress away, Nychelle arched against him.

Suddenly it was as though they had both lost all restraint. Arms tight around each other, their bodies moved in concert, their fiercely demanding kisses whipping the flames of arousal to an inferno.

Continue reading
THE NURSE'S PREGNANCY MIRACLE
Ann McIntosh

Available next month
www.millsandboon.co.uk

LET'S TALK

Romance

For exclusive extracts, competitions
and special offers, find us online:

f facebook.com/millsandboon

⊙ @millsandboonuk

🐦 @millsandboon

Or get in touch on 0844 844 1351*

For all the latest titles coming soon, visit
millsandboon.co.uk/nextmonth